PU...

HORROR STORIES to Tell in the DARK

Anthony Masters is well known as an adult and children's novelist, short-story writer and biographer. He won the John Llewellyn Rhys Memorial Prize for his novel *The Seahorse*. He also works directly with children in his Book Explosion events on both sides of the Atlantic. These uniquely devised workshops bring together writing, drama games, mime, improvisation and adventure training.

His approach to encouraging children to write – and read – has always been to open up their imaginations in a number of very different ways, and in his workshops children take part in simulated creative-writing activities. He has worked with children for many years both in schools and at arts festivals, and is also a regular writer-in-residence for Arts Council Bookweeks and Arts Days.

CONTENTS

A light, scudding breeze blew over Long Heath Lake and the campfire flames flickered uneasily. Suppose a real gale gets up, thought Hannah. Suppose the fire goes out and the tents are blown away. If that happened, they would really have a survival course on their hands. Everything's fine, she told herself. The night had been planned weeks ago, and all ten of them had been looking forward to getting away. They'd decided to sit round the fire telling horror stories tonight. Now Hannah was not so sure. Her eyes roved around the lake on the edge of Dartmoor and watched the water swirl and eddy as the little night breeze sharpened. She shuddered; suddenly she felt uneasy. In her mind's eye, Hannah saw another stretch of water, but this time it was black and deadly calm, without even a ripple to spoil its oily, treacherous surface.

'Are you ready?' asked Jamie, looking up at his sister in

I

expectation, his arms clasping his knees. Around the crackling wood he could see the others, their faces flushed by the flames, their eyes hopeful, anticipating.

And now Hannah's grim memory of the reservoir brought the whole story into focus.

1

THE DEATH TREE

Gwyn, my Welsh cousin, stared at Alun floating face down in the shallows. His body was almost completely still, one arm reaching out towards the muddy bank, fingers splayed as if he had drowned while making one last desperate attempt to reach safety. In fact, it looked as if he had almost succeeded, for there was dank grass between his fingers, and what Gwyn thought might be mangled clover.

The others, Thomas and Danny, had drowned in separate incidents last year; despite the warning notices and thick barbed wire, they had somehow still managed to penetrate the barriers, apparently then to fall into the deadly cold water of the abandoned reservoir.

But Gwyn knew better. The deaths were not accidental.

Alun had gone missing yesterday. The police divers had begun their search late this afternoon only for it to be called off as darkness fell. Gwyn had been sure that his friend would be found in the reservoir eventually, and, sure enough, here he was, floating like a doll, the backs of his hands bloated grey-green in the cold moonlight. Three down. One to go. Gwyn was the only survivor.

Of course, there had been rational explanations and several long newspaper articles. Now what were they going to think, wondered Gwyn. He could imagine the headlines – BLACKWATER CLAIMS THIRD

VICTIM. ANOTHER RESERVOIR DROWNING. COUNCIL INSISTS REDUNDANT RESERVOIR FULLY SECURE – but who would be farsighted enough to realize that *he* might be next? No one, he supposed, for he daren't tell Mum.

Gwyn looked down again at Alun's body and a sob rose in his throat. He was not exactly afraid, for although he had the deadening certainty that he, too, would eventually be floating there, he somehow felt it was not going to be yet. He was numb; all his emotions seemed to be on hold, and he continued to stare down at Alun as if he was a lump of driftwood.

Thomas had drowned at the beginning of last year; Danny six months later and now Alun – how long was it? About eight months. There was no regular interval to the executions, for that was what they were. Gwyn didn't have the slightest doubt about that.

The two previous inquests had recorded 'Death by Misadventure', and the police attitude was that Thomas and Danny were truants and tearaways – the kind of kids who insisted on courting danger. Despite the wire, they had broken into the reservoir and had somehow drowned as a result of a stupid dare. Well, thought Gwyn, it's true – we've all been tearaways: bunking off school, misbehaving, being irresponsible. The victims, as well as Gwyn, lived on Beamish, a rundown council estate where there was joyriding, breaking-in and general mayhem, but that was no excuse, their headteacher had recently told him and Alun. 'You've got to pull yourselves together, lads. I know the conditions you're living in aren't ideal, but that's no excuse to go on behaving like you are. Look what's happened to your mates by breaking and entering. Isn't that enough warning for you?'

Mr Placton had continued talking for some time, but

Gwyn hadn't really been listening. He had simply gone on thinking about the drownings and how he couldn't accuse Silas James because he had no evidence and he had told so many lies all the time he had been at school that no one would possibly believe anything he had said – particularly accusations of murder.

He had accepted Thomas's death as an accident, but Danny's had made Alun and him suspicious, and the more they talked about it the more their sense of foreboding had increased. Gwyn remembered all too clearly a conversation they had had together behind the youth club, just after Danny had been found in the reservoir.

'Do you think it's him?' Gwyn had asked.

'Magog's father? Don't be daft,' Alun had sneered, determined to deny it all, but Gwyn knew that he was just keeping the nightmare at bay.

'They were close.'

'Magog – it was an accident. He was running – and he went off the cliff.'

'Running away from us,' Gwyn reminded him.

'It was a game.'

'Was it? That's not what his dad thought.'

'He's cranky.'

'He was right – we were chasing him.' Gwyn was determined to be realistic.

'Look – that place is dangerous.' Alun began to try and justify the situation, as he always did. 'There was a petition – do you remember? But the Council said it would cost too much to drain the reservoir when it closed, so they put up the wire and kept Mr James on to look after the place.'

'He's so weird though, isn't he?'

'He says he can't cope.' Alun was insistent. 'Not if kids keep busting in. The water's deep right away – no use trying to paddle.'

'Who was paddling?' It was only then that Gwyn had seen the real fear in Alun's eyes – the knowledge that he had been anxious all along. More than anxious.

'Look, Gwyn – you know what Thomas and Danny were like. Always daring each other about the night swim.'

'That's what the police latched on to,' pointed out Gwyn angrily. 'It was an excuse, that's all. A way of neatening it all up.'

'But we *were* always daring each other. You had to swim to the island and bring back a branch of that weird tree – the one that doesn't seem to grow anywhere else.'

Gwyn nodded. He was sure it didn't. They had called it the Death Tree; with its forked branches and withered, shrunken trunk, the tree had always reminded Gwyn of some plastic foliage that advertised the local Garden of Remembrance in the undertaker's window. The sombre shop front, with the undertaker's name in huge gold letters, was situated at the end of the small North Wales town they had all lived in throughout their short lives. Gwyn hated passing it on his way to school. It seemed to make the start of each weekday even more depressing.

'That swim was never on though,' retorted Gwyn. 'Neither of them ever had the nerve to do it.'

It was true – none of them had ever brought back a forked branch. The tree was the only living thing on the tiny island which was stacked with the rusty machinery that had once operated the old sluice gates which were now permanently closed, keeping in the stale, dark water that smelled of rotting weed and dead bodies. Dead bodies? Shock waves ran through Gwyn for the first time and the ghostly conversation with Alun faded away down the channels of time until it was just a faint

6

echo, as withered and lifeless as the solitary tree. The Death Tree they had all dared each other to reach.

Gwyn looked down again at Alun's drowned figure, which moved slightly, pushed by some undetectable swell. There was no wind – so what could have done it? Could there be sluggish currents out there in the still water? Might there be some indefinable undertow? Gazing down at Alun it seemed impossible that he could ever have been alive; impossible to think of dead, drowned Alun moving, swimming. Gwyn's head reeled. *Could* he have been trying to get to the island? To the Death Tree? Was there an ordinary explanation for all three of his friends' deaths after all? Could it really have been just a stupid test of bravery? He knew that Thomas, Danny and Alun had all prided themselves on their courage, their guts, being macho. After all, they didn't have much else going for them. They weren't that bright, or that good at sport. And there wasn't much at home for any of them. All they had in the way of excitement was a challenge.

Suddenly, threateningly, Gwyn remembered the obsessive conversations they had all had about the Death Tree – even wimpish Magog.

'I'll get there one of these days,' Thomas had promised.

'I'll bring back a branch,' Danny had insisted.

'I'll manage somehow,' said Alun, who was the weakest swimmer of them all. 'I can float on my back.'

'Why don't we all do it together?' Gwyn had suggested.

But none of them would agree. 'That would just be a laugh,' Thomas had said. 'We want a dare. You have to swim on your own in the dark – and bring back a branch of the Death Tree. That takes *real* guts.'

Of course, the challenge had been much discussed by

7

the police and also at school, and dire warnings against further attempts had repeatedly been made. Nevertheless, the reservoir had already claimed three lives – four if you counted Magog, who hadn't been able to swim anyway. Maybe that's why he drowned so quickly, thought Gwyn, yet he had always believed that even someone who couldn't swim surfaced at least once. He shuddered at the memory: Magog had definitely gone straight down.

Gwyn was loath to leave Alun, so he sat on the high ledge above him and contemplated the ultimate question. Had he been trying to reach the Death Tree, or had he been murdered by Silas James in revenge for his son's death? If Silas had murdered all three of them was he therefore next on the list? It was impossible to say.

Gwyn froze. He was sure that he had heard something move in the density of the trees. His whole body tensed and he began to feel slightly sick, but then he sharply told himself he was so scared that his imagination would leap to any conclusion.

For the first time, the terror swamped him to such an extent that he could hardly breathe. He didn't want to die like the others; he desperately wanted to live – yet he felt himself to be rooted to the spot, locked into his fear, unable to put one foot in front of the other. He wondered wildly if this was like being in a coma: so aware, so frightened inside, but unable to communicate with those outside.

Gwyn was sure he could hear the step again. Now he was positive that he couldn't be fooling himself, certain that someone was walking softly and purposefully towards him.

'Who's there?' he whispered.

Silence.

'Who's there?'

'You're next.' The words shattered the still night.

'*What?*'

'You're going to die – like the others.'

'Who are you?'

There was no reply, but Gwyn knew the voice belonged to Silas James, the reclusive caretaker of the reservoir, the father of poor, gawky, frightened Magog – the boy they had all bullied so unmercifully; the boy they had driven to his death.

'Mr James?'

There was no reply.

'Mr James?'

Again no response. The man was playing with him – just as they had teased and tormented his son.

'I'm sorry,' Gwyn pleaded into the void. 'I'm really sorry. I didn't know he'd run over the cliff –'

'You'll repent.'

'Yes. You bet I will –' Gwyn gabbled out, seizing any chance he could.

'Your death will be the final atonement.'

'No –'

The man came out of the trees, tall and gaunt as the pines. Silas James.

He was dressed in a jerkin and corduroy trousers tucked into wellington boots. He had a long narrow face with large, troubled eyes. I can outrun him, thought Gwyn. I've got to. But when he looked at James more carefully he could see that he was more powerfully built than he had previously thought and was walking straight towards him. What was worse, Gwyn still felt completely frozen to the spot.

'You killed Magog.' He was very close now, and spoke softly, in a matter of fact way. There was no expression in his voice.

'No.'

'You killed him.'

'He fell over the cliff – into the water. It was an accident. We couldn't find him.' Gwyn was gabbling now, the words tumbling over each other, but still he couldn't move. Desperately he tried to will himself to run. He was fast on his feet. What was holding him? He looked into Silas James's eyes as challengingly as he could, and saw they were a milky grey – like the soft sheen of moonlight.

'You'll swim for the tree.'

'Me?'

'You knew he couldn't swim. That's why he was so afraid of you. He used to say, "They'll make me swim to the tree – and I'll drown."'

'No –'

Silas James walked a couple of steps closer until they were both almost touching.

'So *you'll* swim.' His voice was slow and monotonous as if he was rehearsing well-worn words.

'But I can't. It's too far. I'll drown.'

'Like the others?'

'You made *them* swim?'

'That's what it was all about, wasn't it? It won't be easy. The water drags you down. It's thick and syrupy. Dead.'

'Dead? Water can't be dead.' Gwyn knew now that Silas James was crazy – his only hope was to keep him talking.

'The water died when the reservoir closed. It's never changed, never filtered, never fed.' For the first time his monotonous voice rose to a higher pitch. 'That's why I can't find him.'

Find him?

'They never recovered Magog's body. It's still down there.'

Of course – Gwyn had almost forgotten that. However intensely the divers had searched, no one had been able to recover him. Maybe the water was too deep or murky.

'So I want you to find my son.'

'How could I? How could I find him?' Fighting back his hysteria Gwyn tried to reason with Silas James, but he knew he didn't stand a chance. The man was in the grip of obsession. Gwyn backed away a few paces, but his steps only brought him nearer to the ledge above the water.

'You'll bring him back.' Silas's voice was absurdly confident. 'He'll be by the tree.'

'On the *island*?' Gwyn was incredulous. 'Why should Magog be there?' He knew he couldn't keep his persecutor talking much longer, but he had to try. 'No one ever made it to the island. It's too far.'

'Magog got there. He was better than any of you. He'll be there.'

'How can you be so sure?'

'I am sure. *You've* got to reach him.' Without hesitation, Silas James grabbed Gwyn's shoulders and forced him back. 'Find me Magog,' he demanded. 'Find him.' Effortlessly, he hurled Gwyn into the dark waters of the reservoir.

Gwyn went under immediately, smelling something metallic, cleaving the heavy liquid which resembled molten lead. Silas James was right, he thought. The water *has* died and it was now like a clinging shroud. Somehow he clawed his way to the surface and hung on to a stunted bush that grew at the water's edge. Gwyn looked up into the milky, determined eyes.

'Please –'

'Go to the island.'

'I won't make it.'

'You must.'

With the strength of the damned, Gwyn heaved himself up towards the ledge, clinging to an old tree root. Then he fell back with an agonized cry as Silas James stepped on his fingers, and went into the fetid water for the second time.

Gwyn surfaced again, choking, for the evil stuff was clogging his mouth. It didn't feel like water – more like slurry. He looked up at Silas James.

'Swim,' he said. 'Get to the island. Find Magog.'

Gwyn swam, knowing he was going to die. For a while he pulled himself through the leaden water, keeping his head well up, staring at the sky. Feeling quite detached, he noticed that the clouds seemed to be moving very quickly, flashing over the face of the pale moon. Then he looked ahead to the island, which seemed very small – a dot on this black ocean – and a long way off. A wave of fear surged inside him, but Gwyn continued to strike out, his arms already stiff and sore, occasionally looking back to the outcrop where Silas James stood, a silent, immovable, spectral figure watching his slow progress.

Gwyn knew that if he could just get himself into some kind of rhythm and reach the island, at least he could stay until daylight. Surely someone would come eventually.

A numbing pain had now seized his arms and legs, and every movement he made seemed impossibly painful. Out here, the water was colder, and the rank, rotting smell had become even more pungent. Occasionally, however stiffly he held his head up, the heavy water touched his lips, and once he swallowed some. It tasted acrid.

Now it was being forced into his mouth, trickling down his throat, the stench of it in his nostrils, the taste making him want to vomit. But if he *was* sick, Gwyn knew that he would take in more water. And if he did that, he knew he would begin to drown.

Miraculously, Gwyn became aware that the dark shape of the tiny island with its sentinel tree was now not so far off. He saw the branches were gnarled, crooked, almost grotesquely contorted; and dimly, very dimly, he could see limp-looking white flowers. He imagined touching them and finding them soft and rubbery in his hands, like dead moths.

He was within metres now. Feeling a rush of elation, Gwyn turned to see Silas James still standing there and a surge of defiance filled him. He would get to the island and begin the waiting game – and definitely, quite definitely, he would out-wait him.

The last few metres were long and arduous and the muscles in Gwyn's arms ached so much that he thought they would burst with the pain, but he slogged on until his feet brushed the bottom and he struggled up, his legs shaking so that he could hardly stand. Shivering, but with a feeling of ultimate triumph, Gwyn staggered up the short, pebbly shore, avoided the dark rusting machinery and fell on to rank grass – and something else soft. Then he saw that he had stumbled into a slight dip in the ground and was lying on top of a pile of rags. Rags?

Clouds raced away from the moon and the hard, pale light illuminated a sweater and jeans. Inside the clothes were bones. Skeletal hands – and a skull with a few strands of mousy brown hair still clinging to its cranium. All that was left of Magog James.

With a whimper of revulsion, Gwyn rolled away into short, wiry grass. How had Magog's corpse remained here undiscovered all this time? Why didn't the divers find him? Then he remembered the floods of last winter and how the sterile waters of the reservoir had been temporarily refreshed by the incessant rain – and how the little island and its Death Tree had been submerged. Was this stirring of the elements responsible for lifting Magog from his watery hiding place to rest where he now was? Would the discovery of what was left of his corpse placate his father, who had hardly shifted his watching position since Gwyn had begun his swim?

He staggered to his feet and waved, but Silas James didn't wave back. Gwyn turned to the Death Tree and, for a reason he didn't really understand, gently touched its white flowers. They were silky smooth and slightly moist – highly unpleasant to the touch. Nevertheless, he grabbed a bunch of them, finding them curiously resistant, and scattered them over Magog's skull. They seemed to cling there, covering the eye sockets.

'I'm sorry,' Gwyn whispered. 'I'm sorry for what we did.'

Then slowly and purposefully he plunged back into the tenacious grip of the water, realizing he had to return to Silas with the news.

The swim back seemed easier, as if he was pushing the leaden liquid aside and it was no longer resisting him quite so much. Still Silas James stood on the outcrop, neither welcoming nor rejecting. Gwyn pushed on, almost hopeful, in a muddled, exhausted sort of way. Well – he'd found Magog, hadn't he? Wouldn't Silas be pleased – even grateful – to give Magog a decent burial at last? But as he came closer to the mainland, Gwyn was not so sure, and when he eventually hung on to the tree root, gasping, panting and wheezing, his original paralysing fear gripped him again.

'Mr James?'

The man bent down and rested on one knee, his washed-out eyes on Gwyn's. 'Well?'

'He – he's there.'

There was a long silence. 'Magog?'

'His remains. They're on the island. Maybe they got washed up there in the floods. You could get a boat. Take him away.'

'He's better there,' said Silas James quietly.

'I covered his face with flowers. It was all I could do.'

'It's not enough.' The voice was coldly stern.

'What else –'

'Not enough.' Silas James leant over and with considerable strength loosened Gwyn's rigid grip.

'Let me up,' he pleaded.

'You're the last one. You have to die. Like Magog.'

'No.'

But Silas James pushed him away, harder this time, and as his hand finally slipped away from the root, the deadly fatigue returned and Gwyn sank back under the leaden and foul-smelling water. He broke surface again.

'Please.' Gwyn scrabbled for a hold. 'You've *got* to let me up.'

As he went down again, Gwyn's exhaustion increased and now his whole body felt as heavy as the deadly water itself. Struggling, knowing that he couldn't fight back much longer, he made one last grab at Silas James as he leant forward. His hand grasped Silas's hard bony arm. Their eyes met for a split second and then Silas pitched forward and fell into the water, sinking immediately. Gwyn dragged himself on to the bank, breathless, nauseous. He looked back into the water. Surely the old man had to surface? Then he remembered Magog and looked out towards the Death Tree. It had claimed another victim. Silas had gone straight down.

Gwyn stood there, shivering with cold and shock, and then turned away and walked back to where Alun rested, quietly waiting for him.

★

They looked out at the still water of Long Heath Lake and shuddered.

'Who's got another story?' asked Jamie quickly.

April nodded. 'I've got one,' she said. 'It's all to do with an unreliable car that belonged to a friend of my mother.'

2

InterCity 509

Jenny's mother loved her beaten-up Mini, although it was very old and regularly broke down. Her father had said recently, 'Look, Annie, we're going to have to get rid of that wreck of yours – it's burning money.'

But her mother was adamant. 'Angel's got another few thousand miles in her yet, and I'm going to get her resprayed. I'm *not* selling her, Henry.'

'Selling her?' Jenny's father had closed his eyes. 'She wouldn't fetch a penny. She's only fit for the scrapheap.'

It was a familiar discussion. Usually her parents had a row at this point and Jenny switched off. She knew that her mother loved her car, but secretly she had always thought Angel wasn't a particularly good name for the Mini. Angel was no angel and behaved rather like a spiteful lapdog. Covered in rust and dents, she made a harsh rattling sound all the time; the upholstery was a dirty grey and smelt of rot; the top of the gear stick repeatedly came off and dust blew out of the inadequate heating and cooling system, which seemed to be unbearably hot in summer and freezing cold in winter. But none of these problems really upset Jenny. What terrified her was Angel's continual stalling, which happened at very unpredictable moments and no garage ever seemed able to cure. What was worse, her mother took Jenny to and from school every day, and each morning, and again in the afternoon, Angel had to pass over an unmanned level crossing. Suppose they stalled there of all places, Jenny often thought. Suppose her mother couldn't get Angel started again and one of the InterCity trains hit them?

Originally the horrific idea had started as a mild fantasy, but as time passed and Angel's stalling became more frequent and unpredictable, Jenny's fears became an obsession. She dreaded each day her mother took her to school.

What was worse, Jenny began to have a repetitive nightmare: Angel had stalled on a level crossing and an InterCity express was hurtling towards them. She was sitting beside her mother, who apparently couldn't see the oncoming train and kept saying to Angel – as she often did in real life – 'Have a little rest now – don't get worked up; have a little rest until you feel better.' Then she would turn to the panic-stricken Jenny and say, 'It's no good shouting, dear. Angel won't start till she's ready. You know that.'

'There's a train coming!' Jenny would scream.

'Well – it'll have to wait, dear. Angel's not nearly ready yet.'

Jenny could see the number on the front of the fast-approaching diesel – 509. She kept trying to tell her mother, but she was still talking to Angel and wouldn't look up.

'Start the engine!' screamed Jenny.

'She's not ready yet –'

'Now! Start the engine now!'

The 509 was almost on them and she could see the driver's startled face. Wasn't he familiar? Wasn't he her father? It was always at this point that she woke up, sweating, but temporarily relieved to find that she was back in snug reality. But this feeling only lasted seconds, as she realized that soon it would be time for school and Angel would be spluttering her way towards the un-manned crossing.

★

'Mum —'

'Yes, dear?' Her mother, glasses pushed down to the end of her nose, was studying the newspaper and eating toast. Her father had gone to the office in his brand-new BMW. Jenny was feeling more panicky than ever. The dream had occurred four nights in a row now, and each time the terror had mounted. She was becoming increasingly afraid to go to sleep.

'You've got to have a new car.'

'Mmm?'

'You're not listening.' Jenny accused her irritably.

Her mother reluctantly put down the paper, took off her glasses, and rather wearily ran a hand through her long, brown, straight hair — the kind of hair that fell thickly round her shoulders and that Jenny, who suffered from split, spindly ends, was jealous of. She wasn't exactly thinking about that now, but it did serve to sharpen her irritation.

'What is it?'

'The car.'

'Angel?'

'You've got to sell it, Mum.'

'Never.'

'But why not?'

'You know why not — she was my father's. He drove her right up until he died, and while there's life in Angel, I'm going to keep her sparking.'

'Sparking?' said Jenny nastily. 'That's the last thing she does. She's always stalling. And one of these days there'll be an accident.'

But her mother only picked up the paper again, making a wall between them.

'Mum —'

'I'm not discussing Angel with you. You're as bad as your father.'

'But, Mum –'
'The subject's closed.'

Angel came to a full stop in the High Street and wouldn't start for ages, so when they arrived at the crossing the gates were closed and InterCity 509 was roaring over the tracks, its gleaming coaches dazzling in the early morning sunshine. Jenny found the distorted steel threatening, aggressive; the diesel engine like a hungry mouth; the flashing wheels cruel and predatory. She could imagine Angel flattened beneath the crushing metal and she saw again her father's startled eyes.

Once the train had gone, the gates lifted, Angel's engine started uncertainly and the Mini coughed and clanked its way over the line.

As she started sluggishly to climb the hill to school, Jenny started another attack on her mother, this time a little more desperately.

'Why *don't* you sell her? She's dangerous.'

'Angel?'

'Yes – Angel.'

'The man from Meadows Garage said there was life in her yet, and while there's life there's hope.' Her mother tried to be jolly, but it didn't work.

'He just wants you to spend more money.'

'No – he wants me to buy a new car,' she said with surprising candour. 'But you've got to understand, Jenny.'

'I don't,' she replied bleakly.

'Don't you remember what Grandad said before he died?'

'No.'

'"I want Angel looked after – I want you to remember me when you drive her."'

'He was ill, Mum.'

'That's the point.'

'No it isn't. He didn't know what he was saying.'

'He did, Jenny. I know what he wanted.' Her mother was becoming sad rather than heated.

'Do you really?' Jenny was angry now. She knew she was being unfair, but her fear was greater than her desire not to wound. 'I just think you're putting your life at risk – and mine.'

'Don't be so stupid.' Her mother was stung, surprised at her daughter's vehemence.

'*I'm* not being stupid.'

'Well – I think you are.'

That night Jenny dreamed again, but the nightmare was much worse. This time her mother didn't even attempt to start Angel but simply sat behind the wheel, drinking from a thermos of coffee and reading her newspaper, while InterCity 509 thundered down the track towards them. Jenny could clearly see her father behind the controls and soon he was leaning out of the cab window, screaming at her mother.

She woke up with the 509 still heading towards them, her father making no attempt to put on the brakes.

Jenny lay in bed shaking all over, the sweat dripping into her eyes. The feeling of relief swamped her again and then came the realization that she had to go to school. Where would Angel stall this time? Was *this* the morning when she would come to a grinding halt on the crossing?

She got out of bed and slowly went to the window. The sky was a swollen grey and a heavy drizzle fell on to the misty garden below. Angel was parked outside the garage. Inside lay her father's BMW. That was another point of conflict between her parents, for her mother was always complaining that Angel was left out in the cold and rain while her father insisted his BMW should be kept in the warmth of the garage. So far her mother had lost the battle, although she had fallen back on saying that *this* was the reason Angel kept stalling – that she would be much more reliable if she was kept under cover – a defence that her father derided. Jenny didn't know what to believe; she was simply fed up with her parents' constant arguing as well as being so afraid of Angel's unreliability. The whole business seemed to be circular.

Apprehensively she looked down at the old car, her rusty bodywork saturated and clothed in a blanket of mist. As a result the Mini simply looked not just sulky and disobliging as she often did, but downright vengeful.

The big row broke at breakfast. Mum had overslept, Dad had had to get her out of bed to move Angel so that he could back the BMW out of the garage, but the Mini had refused to start, and Dad had mud on his trousers where he slipped over pushing Angel. He was furious – even more so as she had still refused to start. Mum was defensive and stubborn.

'You've *got* to sell her,' he was saying, spooning cornflakes into his mouth and trying to talk at the same time. 'She's a heap of junk.'

'No.'

'It stands to reason.'

'Reason maybe – but she was my father's.'

'Then turn her into a museum – but don't drive her. And find a field – not the drive.'

'You hate Angel, don't you?' Her mother finally lost her own temper as Jenny sat down at the table.

'She's an utter nuisance.'

The heightened nightmare still fresh in her mind,

Jenny felt completely exhausted.

'Mum –'

'Well?'

'I think Dad's right. You don't have to sell her –'

'No one would want that heap,' put in her father un-helpfully.

'You could keep her somewhere. Put flowers inside her – make her into a memorial for Grandad.'

'No,' her mother rapped. 'Angel stays on the road – just as my father wanted her to.'

'Until she falls apart?' asked Dad, munching toast and still looking furious as he picked at the mud on his trousers.

'Until the garage say she can't go any longer.' There was a sob in her mother's voice now and Jenny took her hand.

'It's just that she might be dangerous.' Somehow she felt she couldn't go as far as telling her about the nightmare. Maybe Dad would laugh, and Mum was certain to get even more upset.

'She's safe.'

'But keeps stopping,' said Jenny as gently as she could.

'And won't start,' put in Dad.

But her mother had had enough. Rising from the table, in a mixture of hurt and anger she shouted, 'Shut up, you two.'

'We're only trying to help –' Jenny began.

'Well, you're *not* helping. Just leave me and Angel alone. I'm going to phone the garage. *You'll* have to take Jenny to school, Henry.'

With that, she went out and banged the door.

At least this is one day when I don't have to dread the crossing, thought Jenny as Dad drove her out of the drive in the BMW, leaving Angel slewed round on the concrete, looking huddled and pathetic now, in the wafts of clearing mist. She glanced back again just as they turned the corner and had the strange, unsettling feeling that the old car was looking far from angelic: her twisted fender gave the appearance of a cynical smile.

Neither father nor daughter spoke as the BMW drove down the High Street towards the crossing. In fact, Jenny was so exhausted that she must have dozed off as the car approached the rails. When she opened her eyes, the BMW was straddling the crossing and had come to a halt.

'Dad –'

'Shan't be a sec.'

'What are you doing?'

'What does it look like? I'm trying to start the car.'

'But –'

'For some unaccountable reason, she's stalled. It's never happened before.'

He turned the ignition again and again but nothing happened. Then Jenny saw the train coming; it was hurtling down on them – the InterCity 509.

'Get out!' her father yelled.

But when she tried the door it wouldn't open.

'The child-lock –' he screamed, but it was too late. The 509 tore into the BMW with a rending, screaming tearing of metal.

There was a long silence, after April's story. The assembled company by the dark lake was completely motionless.

'Who's got the next story?' Hannah half whispered.

'I have,' said Anne.

3

SOUL SUCKER

I was staying in a monastery near Moscow with my dad. He's an expert restorer and he'd been invited to work on some religious pictures called icons in this very old place on the marshes. It was a lovely building, dedicated to St Nicholas, but it was on a small island and always seemed full of mist and marsh gases. When we were there it was the dead of winter, and the caretaker cut the peat from the swamps to burn on the guest-house fire. 'Dead of winter.' People often say that, but I'll always associate those words with the St Nicholas monastery. The very stones that made up the building exuded a damp, rotting smell.

My father and I were there for two weeks, but the time passed so slowly that it seemed like an eternity. What was more, we rarely saw anyone: the icons had been laid out in the dining-room of the guest house for Dad to work on as we weren't allowed to go into the monastery itself because the order of monks there was a closed, silent one. Only the Abbot was allowed to chant prayers and sing Mass. He had the deepest voice I've ever heard; I used to listen to him regularly throughout the day and night, when he often kept me awake with his plaintive sound.

Once Dad and I went to a Russian Orthodox Mass in the monastery's public chapel, where a local choir sang while, in a screened-off side chapel, the silent monks of St Nicholas would gather and the Abbot would lead the service.

★

For the first few days I was very lonely as I prowled around the grounds. The monastery was small, with crosses surmounting the domed roofs. There was a large front door and then a high, grey wall jutted out, enclosing the remainder of the building, and I had the odd feeling that all this desolate brick was to keep the monks in – not to keep the public out. The wall extended beyond the monastery, over some long grass and then into a sad little woodland of spiky trees and stunted bushes. There was a door in the wall that was usually closed, but on one occasion I noticed that it was slightly ajar – as if for a breath of fresh air.

Summoning up all my courage I went to take a peek, but all I could see was part of a cloister. Next time I passed, the door was firmly closed, and I wondered uneasily if the silent monks had seen me spying on them.

Then I met Igor, and what had been simply a sense of isolation and foreboding became raw fear.

Igor was the caretaker's son and was studying at a Moscow boarding-school, where he was learning every subject in English and only came home at weekends. He was short and belligerent-looking and at first I took against him, but once I'd spoke to him I realized that Igor was as lonely as I was and desperately wanted to make friends.

We first met by the old, dried-out fishponds – another desolate sight at St Nicholas – and Igor asked me if I was happy. I shook my head.

'It's so spooky – and my father's busy all day. There's nothing to do.'

'Why's it spooky?' he asked.

'The monks. They scare me. I looked in – when the door in the wall was open – and it was awful.'

'Awful?'

'Dead and dry and dusty.'

'You shouldn't have trespassed,' he said sternly. 'It's forbidden.'

'Hasn't your father *ever* been in there?' I pressed him, and suddenly realized that I had become very curious.

'Of course not.'

'And you?'

'Never.' Igor sounded really scared. 'That door should never have been open; it very rarely is.'

'Don't they have *any* visitors?' I inquired quietly.

'No.'

'What about supplies?'

'My father leaves everything on a huge trolley in the public chapel. Then he goes away and one of the monks pushes it back into the compound.'

'The compound? That's a terrible word,' I admonished.

'Nevertheless, that's what we call it.' He paused rather hesitantly and then began to speak rapidly and urgently. 'You mustn't, under any circumstances, go through that door.'

'I was only looking –'

'Looking becomes wanting. Other people have gone in –' Igor whispered.

'What happened to them?' Then I realized what he might be trying to tell me. 'You mean they never came back?'

'They came back,' he said hesitantly. 'But they were changed.'

'Changed?' Why couldn't he get to the point?

'Mentally.'

'How? Was it obvious?' This was all so unnerving and so unexpected that I wondered if Igor was teasing me, but when I looked into his haunted eyes I could see he was serious. I hardly knew him, but already we had formed a terrible bond.

'They just shut themselves away inside as if they'd had something taken away.'

I lay awake all night. What had been taken from the people who had trespassed into the monastery? The dreadful thoughts rattled round in my head making sleep impossible, so eventually I rose and went to the window.

The grounds of the guest house were bathed in a sharp, white light, and the moon rose overhead, looking pale and sickly. Everything seemed to have a slightly diseased air. The trees looked bent and brittle, the grass jaundice-yellow and the wall surrounding the monastery a deathly white. There were no stars in the sky – only racing clouds – and from somewhere a mournful nightjar called, repeating the cry again and again. It was as if the world outside had turned sour and lost all its colour and warmth and vivacity. It looked as if something had sucked out all the goodness and left only badness. I tried to dismiss the idea, but it wouldn't go away.

The next morning I looked for Igor, but the caretaker told me curtly that he was ill. Disappointed and lonely, I wandered around disconsolately for a while, trying to think what I was going to do that day. As usual my father was poring over the icons, so in the end I decided to knock on the door of the caretaker's flat and see if I could at least speak to Igor. There was no answer for a long time and then the bolts were drawn back and his mother stood on the threshold. She looked afraid.

'Can I see Igor?'

She stared at me uncomprehendingly, her eyes red and full of tears.

'Igor?' I tried again.

His mother nodded and led me through the cramped little apartment until I came to a small room whose walls were covered with the colours and photographs of a football team. Igor was in bed, lying on his back, his face ashen and expressionless except for his eyes which stared feverishly up at me.

Directly his mother left the room, Igor whispered, 'I thought you'd come.'

'What's happened?' I asked. 'Are you ill?'

'No. I went into the monastery.'

I was horrified. 'Why? I thought you said –'

'I felt this – urge.'

'Yes.' I nodded. 'I felt that too. Then I looked out of the window last night and had this weird feeling that the earth was being drained.'

'Something in there.' His voice was now just a croak.

'What do you mean?' I couldn't remember a time when I had ever been so afraid.

'The door was open. I felt as if I was being invited in.' I had to strain to hear what he was saying. 'Inside everything was very plain and bare, and nothing was growing – not even a tree. The ground was covered with a kind of ash and I couldn't even see any grass. What's more, there didn't seem to be any paint on the buildings, and when I caught sight of one of the monks he was white and bald – he didn't even have any eyebrows.' Igor coughed, and for a moment I didn't think he was going to be able to carry on, but somehow he continued. 'I hid for a while, feeling terrified, but still curious. Then I heard a sound – a sort of sucking sound.'

I shuddered. 'Where was it coming from?'

'The bell tower. So I went over, opened the door, checked no one was looking and began to climb up.' The whisper became even fainter. 'There was slime on the stairs. I slipped on it and when I touched the stuff it was warm. Immediately I felt I couldn't go on, so I came down and opened the door in the wall again. My legs became weaker and weaker and I only just made it back.' He paused. 'When I went to bed I dreamt, and the dream kept recurring. I'm going back in there. Up those stairs – through that slime. Someone's calling me.'

'You've got a fever.' I tried to soothe him.

'Someone's calling,' he repeated, and his pale features twisted in an agony that was terrible to see.

'You don't know what you're saying –' I pleaded with him frantically, but it was no good.

'I've got to go,' he whispered again and again, and eventually his mother came and ushered me away. Because she spoke no English and I had no Russian it was impossible for us to talk about Igor and the call that he claimed had come for him, but I knew by instinct that she was as terrified as I was.

I went for a walk in the pine woods later that morning and then sat on top of the hill, looking down at the interior of what I now called the forbidden monastery. I had climbed through deep snow, but the morning sun was sparkling on the soft white carpet which gave off a curiously unearthly radiance. There was nothing much to be seen in the cloisters below: the occasional monk walking slowly amongst the painted columns, a cat running towards the bell tower and then the mournful deep sound of the Abbot singing the midday office. Then I saw the cat return, and even from my vantage point I could make out that the creature had changed colour from jet-black to a curiously transparent grey. I stared down, wondering if I was mistaken or if the snow glare was making my eyes deceive me. But no – the cat was now ash-white.

Suddenly I saw a monk walk slowly away from the cloister and then break into a run, and strained my eyes to see what was going on. He looked pallid like the cat as he bent over the creature, stroking its fur and looking up at the bell tower. Even from a distance I could feel the hatred in him, see his anger. Then he did a very curious thing: moving quickly across the quadrangle, he hurried to the door in the wall and opened it slightly. Picking up the cat, he hurried back into the building.

I slid and stumbled down the hillside, possessed by an unsettling certainty that the door was being deliberately left open, and as I came nearer I distinctly saw Igor walking unsteadily out of the guest house and towards the monastery wall. Bursting into a stumbling run I shrieked out his name, but I was still too far away for him to hear me.

As I tumbled through the snow, mile upon mile of pine woods seemed to flash past me, a huge wilderness where anything could happen, anything could lurk in the dead ground under the trees. Only rarely would a penetrating sunbeam dart through the foliage and I imagined things moving away, seeking shadows and darkness. The images kept coming into my mind as if they were some kind of transmitted warning.

Gasping for breath, I arrived back in the valley with a great feeling of despair. Then I saw that the door was still open.

Cautiously, but without hesitation, I walked into the monastery. The early afternoon sun filtered from dark clouds overhead and shafts of ancient sunlight, mellow and glowing, slanted across the quadrangle. There was no one around and a thick silence filled the air. Then a single bell began to toll and beneath the sound I heard an odd fluttering of what seemed to be dry wings. Gradually, the terror grew inside me until I could hardly breathe. Nevertheless, I pressed on, staring round to see if I was unobserved until, keeping to the shadows, I walked quickly towards the tower.

I opened the sombre wooden door, and saw a flight of worn stone stairs. I was just about to ascend when I heard the sound of running steps outside and froze, desperately looking around me for a hiding-place. There was nowhere, and seconds later I saw the flushed white face of a tall man with a bald head.

He gazed at me in silence, and I could see his skin was so stretched and grey that it seemed to be flaking away. 'I am the Abbot,' he said at last, his voice thin and weak. 'You are trespassing.'

'I'm looking for Igor,' I stuttered.

'You are trespassing,' he repeated.

'I have to find Igor – he's ill.'

'He's going to die.'

'No –' I was horrified.

'There is nothing you can do to save him.'

I tried to run up the stairs, but the Abbot grabbed my arm and held it tightly. 'I cannot allow any more sacrifice.'

'Sacrifice?' I was completely bewildered now.

'A young child's soul contains less sin. His appetite is sharper for these – like we enjoy young lamb.'

'I don't know what you're talking about.'

'Come with me. I will show you. Then you must go.'

I followed the Abbot to the main monastery building with its two domes. We climbed up a long flight of stairs until we came to a circular room whose only furnishings were a heavily decorated chair and a foot-stool.

'Sit down, child.'

I did as I was told, but I felt a burning restlessness. Why was Igor going to die? There must be *some* way of saving him.

'Why was the door in the wall left open?' I demanded.

'My brothers have been – weak.'

'I thought the monastery was closed to outsiders.'

'It is. But my brothers, like me, are being drained.'

With renewed shock I remembered the colourless landscape of my dreams. 'Drained?'

'It will end in fire,' he said slowly.

I stared at the Abbot uncomprehendingly as he continued, his long grey head turned towards me but his jaundiced eyes staring out of the round window towards the bell tower. 'Some years ago one of our brothers lost his faith and he began to study alchemy. He wanted to find powers denied to him by God. He sought union with darkness – with Satan.' He paused, but I didn't dare interrupt, despite my desperation for Igor.

'The devil's powers need sustenance – the sustenance of the soul,' he continued.

'You mean –' I broke into involuntary speech, trying to understand the full horror of what the Abbot was trying to tell me.

'I mean that our brother feeds off the human soul.'

I stared at him, unable to take in the enormity of what he was saying. 'Did he gain any powers?' I said at last.

'He thought he would gain more – perhaps in the end be as all-seeing, all-embracing as God himself – but the Devil ensnared him.'

'In the bell tower?'

'So far we have kept his – his form to ourselves, but we are growing too weak. He is feeding off us, you must understand. Then one of the brothers opened the door in the wall. He was hoping the curious would enter and there would be some alleviation to our suffering.'

'You mean – that the brother would feed off them instead?'

'He was very wrong.' At last the Abbot looked me in

the eye and I could see his shame and guilt. 'I cannot let this happen any longer.' He rose to his feet. 'I will show you and then you must go.'

'Not without Igor,' I insisted.

'I am afraid that is impossible.'

'I must rescue him – before it's too late.'

'It *is* too late.'

In the dying light I could see a dark shape in the bell tower, and hear, through the half-open window, the rustling of wings. I turned to the Abbot, but he put a finger to his lips and beckoned me to follow him downstairs.

'The monks will distress you, child. They are far more drained than I. Prepare yourself.'

I tried to steel myself against what I was going to see, but when he threw open the double oak doors and I stared down at the things sitting behind the table I failed to choke back a scream.

There were some twenty monks on either side of the long, unvarnished table, set with plates of bread and bowls. Some of the men had washed-out complexions and translucent skins, but others were unbearable to look at with their exposed veins and arteries clearly visible. In one man I could see his brain showing through his forehead. The monks did not look up but remained staring down at their plates in humble supplication, and as my scream died away I buried my face in the dusty robe of the Abbot. Then the door opened behind me.

'Don't look,' the Abbot said.

But I had to, for I knew by some sixth sense that Igor wanted me. Wrenching myself from the Abbot's grasp I turned to face Igor.

He was like an anatomical specimen. The thing had feasted on him and I saw Igor's blood thinly circulating around his frame. But what was far worse, there was a terrible emptiness to him: his soul had been sucked dry and all I was looking at was machinery. The bloodless lips moved in his dead white face and the expressionless voice called my name again and again.

What had once been Igor came towards me with hands outstretched. It was only then that I began to run.

I stood trembling outside the still half-open door in the wall of St Nicholas's monastery. Twilight was drifting into darkness now as I watched the Abbot walking towards the bell tower with his arm around what had once been Igor. The rising moon shone right through the boy. Behind them came the monks, holding flaming brands, and slowly the procession disappeared into the tower.

I waited until I heard the roaring sound. Suddenly the whole building was engulfed by fire and smoke as the bell began to toll. The flames leapt and crackled; then the roof fell in, and a creature, half man, half bat, rose from the inferno, its snow-white human head emitting a dreadful cry.

'What's that?' hissed Will, and the bonfire flames rose as he threw a log into them.

'What's what?' said Anne.

Something rustled past in the firelight.

'That's a rat,' said Barry with conviction. The group round the fire huddled together. 'Reminds me of a seaside town I once knew . . .' he continued.

4

RATS

The battered old trawler limped into the harbour when I was fishing on the wall late at night. She was so low in the water that for a moment I wondered if she was going to founder. *Lady Jane* was the name carved on her bows, barely discernible amongst the flaking paint and barnacled hull. Her rigging was rusty, one of the hatches was broken and there was a great gouge on her starboard side.

'Tod's home.' The rough voice of Captain Soames made me start, but I was not particularly surprised at his sudden appearance. The old man haunted the harbour wall and there was rarely a time when he was not wandering about its stained concrete and mooring posts – some of which were split and badly weathered. 'That's bad news,' he added.

'Why?' I asked.

'Swine of a man. Runs the *Lady Jane* single-handed – only because no one would sail with him.'

'How long's he been away?' I said, reeling in my line, knowing full well that I couldn't concentrate while Captain Soames was around. Rumoured to have been in the Royal Navy years ago, he was a permanent fixture in Sungate, knowing all there was to know about the dying trade in the old harbour and the few fishing boats that still actually went to sea for a living.

'Two years. Roaming the coast – picking up contract work where he could.'

Rats

The *Lady Jane* came nearer, easing her way into the harbour with a melancholy blast from her horn. There seemed to be a figure crouched in the wheelhouse, but the perspex was so salt-caked that it was impossible to make it out very well. The wipers had cleared a patch to see through, but the helmsman's vision must have been dangerously limited.

'Those decks are almost awash,' I said.

'Got a leak – maybe the pump's packed up,' the Captain suggested.

'Why did he sail off like that? Isn't this his home port?'

'If you can call this dump a port. Yes – he used to belong here. He was born and bred in the town, but he was a swine,' Captain Soames repeated darkly.

'How do you mean?' I asked, and then hoped the old man wasn't going to ramble. I'd had a sudden desire to go home for tea; the arrival of the *Lady Jane* seemed to have brought a chill to the early autumn evening. I looked down at her, wallowing in the grey-green water, and felt an unreasonable sense of revulsion. There was something menacing about the way she lay so low in the water, as if she was bulging at the seams, heavy with something to hide.

'He beat his wife and kids – and then hated the town because they were taken away from him by the social services. The kids were put in care and his wife went to a shelter, but they've got a house in East Street now and they'll be sorry to see him back. Maybe I should go and alert them.' He paused. 'I wouldn't hang around if I were you – he's a nasty bit of work. Swore vengeance on the whole town –' Captain Soames stopped speaking abruptly as the wheelhouse door opened and a long, lean man with a narrow face appeared. He was dressed in greasy overalls, but it was his presence, like that of his

37

trawler, that was particularly unpleasant. His long features glittered with malevolence, and for a moment I thought it was almost a satisfied malevolence, as if he had come home with a purpose – and that purpose was radiating from him. I stared at him, and as I stood there I was sure that I could hear a horrible scurrying, scratching sound from the hold. Maybe it's all my imagination, I tried to tell myself, but somehow I knew it wasn't.

'Soames,' the man said to the Captain.

'Yes?'

'I remember you.' The sentence was like an accusation, spoken raspingly, mockingly, and with a certain pleasure.

'And I remember you, Tod Marling. You're not welcome in Sungate – and you should know that.'

'You old fool. Always were a bag of wind. I'm back here to claim my own.'

'Your own?'

'Freda and the kids.'

'They're not *yours*.' Soames's voice was more positive and a rush of affection for him filled my heart. I knew the old man was afraid, yet he was still determined to stand up to this long, thin streak of evil. 'You *think* you own them, but they're not your possessions, you know.'

Tod Marling barked with laughter, like a hound scenting blood. 'You're going to regret the way you treated me – all of you in this hole of a town. You deserve plague and pestilence and, believe me, you'll get it.' He laughed uproariously and I suddenly realized that he was more than a little mad.

'You've had a restraining order placed on you,' yelled Soames, suddenly beside himself with hot rage. 'You're not to go near Freda.'

'They can't stop me.'

'I will, though. I'm going to warn them. Come on, young Barry, you're coming with me.'

He didn't have to ask me a second time, for I could see the glazed fury in Tod Marling's eyes and knew for a certainty that he must have come home to Sungate for some terrible revenge.

'He's just a troublemaker,' said Captain Soames as we strode up the hill to the town, but I couldn't help feeling the old man was trying to make light of the situation so that I wouldn't be scared. 'No more, no less. He'll go back to sea.'

'What did he mean about plague and pestilence?' I asked.

'Lot of hot air.'

'You don't reckon there's anything *in* that hold, do you?'

'No, I don't. She's either sprung a leak, or he's caught too many fish,' said the old man briskly, but I didn't feel entirely convinced.

I returned home, had my supper and went to bed, but I lay awake wondering about Tod Marling and his evil eyes, and when I finally drifted into sleep I dreamt of the battered, forbidding old trawler, now so low in the water that its decks were awash.

Next day I went to school, and when I came back I found my mother looking distraught and my younger sister, Stella, morbidly excited.

'What's going on?' I asked at once.

My mother hesitated, but Stella immediately burst into speech. 'Haven't you heard?'

'Heard what?'

'Captain Soames is dead.'

I froze. 'How?' I asked eventually, and then could have kicked myself for heightening Stella's all too obvious dramatic enjoyment.

'Sharon said he was bitten to death.'

'Bitten?'

'Now, we don't know anything of the kind,' my mother intervened angrily. 'You know what Sharon's like – always spreading awful rumours. The poor man probably died of a heart attack. He was very old.'

'But Sharon lives next door to him, and her dad found him. He was all –'

'Be quiet, Stella. Can't you see you're upsetting your brother? Barry was very fond of the Captain.'

Bitten to death, I thought. Why had Tod Marling's trawler been so low in the water – and what was that scampering sound I had heard in her hold?

By the time I reached the harbour, I had convinced myself that I was overreacting. Who on earth would bring in a cargo of rats? The whole idea was completely ridiculous. Mum had to be right and poor old Captain Soames had died of a coronary. He was always wheezing and his pipe had hardly ever been out of his mouth.

The *Lady Jane* was riding surprisingly high in the water and the tide was full. She was locked up and silent, only her mooring lines making a slight creaking sound as she rode up and down by the old seaweed-covered stones of the wall. I watched her until the light faded, trying to think what I should do. Eventually I decided there was nothing I *could* do. After all, I had no evidence whatsoever.

Walking back, I took a short cut through Knot Alley – one of a number of narrow passages running between the old clapboard cottages of Sungate. This was the ancient part; the rest of the town had grown up after the war as a tatty holiday resort and now, with the season over, was mainly boarded up and had an air of melancholy.

My dad is a long-distance truck driver, and we had moved to Sungate from London because it didn't really matter where we lived and Dad had thought a house by the sea would be good for Stella's asthma. Unfortunately, the only place he could afford was Sungate – one of the ugliest towns on the south coast. Its only attraction was the old harbour area which I loved, but there wasn't much of it left and developers were always threatening to knock the rest of it down to provide holiday flats.

I'd always loved lingering in the old alleys: the mixed smells of tar and pitch, fish and cork. That day I poked about amongst the scattered and abandoned old lobster-pots and netting, noticing that there was even the hulk of a sloop, dragged up to dry land and probably forgotten. This was what Captain Soames had also loved about Sungate and a sudden anger at his death flooded my mind. Even if the Captain *had* had a heart attack, maybe it was because Tod Marling had frightened or upset him in some way. My rage increasing, I left the alley and walked past the old cinema that, like the lobster-pots, had been abandoned for many years. The stuccoed façade of the Roxy was peeling, yet there was still a battered poster for a horror movie, *Killer Bees*, stuck firmly to the wall.

I paused for a second as out of the corner of my eye I caught sight of something flashing past. The first sharp pang of fear stabbed at me as I saw it crouched there. A rat. An enormous rat that was watching me from beneath a litter-bin. Its eyes were venomous, but it was the sheer size of the rodent that riveted me. The rat's thin lips were curled back to reveal hideously yellowed fangs and soft pink gums. I stepped back quickly as the vile thing raced past me into a gap under the boarded-up door of the Roxy.

Revolted, I would have liked to run home, but instinctively feeling it must have something to do with Tod Marling and the death of Captain Soames, I climbed over the wall and cautiously edged my way down another alley, this time running *beside* the old cinema. I had to pick my way through old rotting mattresses, a mass of rusty bed-springs, a very ancient mangle and a stinking pile of old newspapers, but eventually I reached the window of the old cinema and found that it was illuminated by the bright neon lights of the supermarket next door. With a grunt of satisfaction I pulled myself up on the ledge – and then felt a crushing sense of anticlimax, for I was looking into the shadowed interior of a derelict office and could see nothing but an old filing cabinet with its drawers pulled out and a stained desk covered with yellowed cinema magazines and handbills. But a door led into the remainder of the building and behind it I was sure that I could see a small, gleaming, beady eye. Did I really have the guts to see if the rats were in the cinema, or wouldn't it be better just to go and ring the police? Surely that was the most sensible move.

I clambered down from the window-ledge – and found myself held in a vice-like grip.

'Curious, son?' rasped Tod Marling, placing his horny hand over my mouth while keeping the crook of his arm around my neck. 'Curiosity killed the cat.'

I kicked and struggled as hard as I could, but Marling was strong and wiry, so I soon became exhausted.

'Come and see my friends,' Marling whispered. 'They're hungry, you know, desperately hungry. But I've promised them the feast of a lifetime. You'll simply be the aperitif – just a minuscule bite for them all. Trouble is, my family aren't civilized. I don't mean Freda and the kids – I mean my *real* family.' He gave a little whimper of quickly suppressed laughter.

He's crazy all right, I thought. What am I going to do now? I caught a glimpse of the interior of the supermarket. There was a stack of cornflakes packets and a worn-out old lady pushing an overloaded trolley, and faintly, very faintly, I could hear the music that was being played in the store. What was the tune? My mind insisted on trying to remember – anything to block out what was going to happen. Oh yes, it was 'The Happy Wanderer'. *Valderee, valderaa,* sang the tinny choir, *With my knapsack on my back.* It was all so ordinary, so familiar in the supermarket, but out here, I was about to die.

'Once they smell blood,' said Tod Marling, 'my family get very greedy.'

He dragged me, still squirming, through the debris, to the back of the cinema and then thrust me through an open door.

I was standing in some kind of small storage area and there was a musty smell of disuse and something rank. I guessed what it was immediately, as Tod Marling pulled the door behind him until we were both standing in the pitch-darkness.

'We paid Captain Soames a visit last night,' he whispered, the sharp beam from his torch probing in the dark corners. 'Not all of us. Just enough to share a bite.' He gave a raucous little laugh. 'He got to Freda and the kids first – warned them I was coming, so when I arrived they'd done a bunk. Never mind.' He paused reflectively. 'They can't have gone far. They haven't got any money, so I'll catch up with them soon. In the mean time I'm going to set my family on the town – tell them to really live it up. After all, a port's a place to have fun in and my family haven't been to a port in months. They even had to live off each other – and they still do, you know. Mark you, they prefer human flesh.'

He paused again and smiled. 'I trained them into that, you know, when I was in the Friesian Islands. They're wild and remote, so my family grew without being disturbed – without running away from me like my old family does.' He laughed again and the sound was terrible to hear, backed up as it was by the flurried scampering from the main body of the cinema. They must be everywhere, I thought, and when I imagined them swarming over the faded crimson seats I felt horribly sick.

I've got to play for time – got to take him off guard, I thought. Tod Marling, still in his filthy overalls, was standing by the outside door, but there was another door, behind which I could hear them scampering. To get away from Marling I would have to run through there – into the pitch-darkness and the clusters of rancid furry bodies, with their darting teeth and shining boot-button eyes. In the darkness I would find no way out and they would have me down, snapping at me until they buried their decayed teeth in my body.

'How – how did you get them all?'

'Oh, it was easy. The islands are full of them. I collected my family – they didn't collect me.' He gave a little giggle. 'Boats and boatyards, grain silos and deserted farmhouses, barns and cellars – even an old, wrecked cargo ship. I lured them into my hold with hunks of meat – hunks of human meat. They soon got the taste for it and now they won't have anything else. My family don't scavenge any more; they wait to be shown.' Again he giggled, and then his humour deserted him. 'This town rejected me – ran me out – I could have been tarred and feathered. So when my family's had their little hors-d'oeuvre I'll release them on Sungate.'

'The pest control people'll soon mop them up,' I said.

'Not before they've spread plague and pestilence.'

'How will they do that?'

'They're disease carriers.' He grabbed my arm and whispered, 'Come and meet them.'

'Wait,' I pleaded.

'But they can't wait. They're hungry.' His breath was as rank as I imagined the rats' would be.

'How did you get them here?'

'Oh, I wanted to find an overnight shelter for us – this seemed the best place.'

'They *followed* you here?' I asked, desperately trying to keep Tod Marling talking.

'I'm the Pied Piper.'

'But how?'

'They know I'm their provider. Even rodents have instincts, you know. I'm their father.' His eyes glittered. 'I'm the rat king.'

You're also crazy. Absolutely stark, staring, raving, horribly crazy, I thought, and I began to shake so much that I could hardly stand. 'Please,' I whispered like a small child. 'Let me go. I won't tell – I promise I won't tell on you.'

'But you will. You will tell,' said Tod Marling, his eyes wide and staring. 'You'll tell Freda and the kids – just like Soames did, won't you?'

'No!' I howled.

'Come on. We've done enough talking, don't you think?'

I began to struggle again, but Marling's grip on my arm was now so fierce that it hurt badly as he propelled me on towards the door that led into the cinema.

Marling switched off the torch and there was an abrupt stillness except for the scraping of a paw, a muffled squeak and a quick movement. But none of this seemed to matter – none of this terrified me as much as the sudden shock of the hundreds and hundreds of eyes glinting in the deep darkness.

'My family,' breathed Tod Marling.

Then he switched on the torch again and its brilliant light swept the serried ranks of rats. They were huge, and the smell of their massed bodies was appalling. My eyes travelled to the half-eaten carcasses amongst them, those weaker rats who had been used as food by the starving cannibals.

'You see how hungry they are,' whispered Marling. 'Just think what they'll do to the good citizens of Sungate. After all, the Captain was only a demonstration – as you'll be. They'll pick your bones in seconds. Do you know what I'm going to do?'

'No,' I stuttered.

'I'm going to prop up your gleaming white skeleton just outside that supermarket. They'll all think it's a joke at first – until it happens to them. When they open at nine, I'll release the rats amongst the shelves. There'll be human fodder first – and then more passive fare.' He laughed again, but this time more calmly, soberly.

By the light of the powerful beam, I could see that we were both standing on the derelict stage of the cinema from which the screen had been removed. Below us the rats waited, packed into the area where the stalls had been. Slowly the beginnings of an idea began to take shape in my mind. I had no idea whether it would work or not, but I knew I had nothing to lose.

'Come on then.' Marling turned to the rats. 'Hello, family. I've got a little present for you. Sorry it's so puny.'

His torch swept their eyes, hopeful and baleful. There was a joyous mass squeal and a moving forward of the tightly packed ranks, as they trod over the half-eaten corpses of their fellows.

Taking him completely by surprise, I shoved Marling as hard as I could and he plunged to the floor, cracking his head as the rats swiftly parted. Almost immediately, blood ran down his forehead and I gasped in mingled relief and horror. This was what I had just planned, but I never thought it would work out so beautifully. Beautifully? Marling sat up, the blood pouring down his face now. The rats squealed, darted and charged. Within seconds Marling was a mass of obscene wriggling brown bodies, whose tails lashed and teeth snapped in ecstasy.

At this point Gill wanted to go home — to forget all about this harrowing party. But glancing around she saw eyes alight with excitement. They were on her now and Gill knew that she would have to prove herself. 'I knew someone who was very sentimental once,' she began. 'At least — that's the way she looked.'

5

A Deprived Child

Mrs Jackson was one of those old ladies who looked as if she could do no harm to anyone. She was a widow; her husband had been dead for many years, her children were grown up, and she devoted herself to good works in the village. She looked like I imagined she was – a sweet, white-haired old lady; round, plump, homely, and dressed in trim little outfits with powder-blue cardigans that matched her eyes, tweed skirts, lisle stockings and sensible shoes. Most of the time she wore tortoise-shell National Health glasses, red mittens in winter and, almost always, lilac gloves in the summer.

Although Mrs Jackson was well into her seventies, there was very little wrong with her except what she called her 'gammy' leg. Whatever it was, she walked with a decided limp and, because we lived next door, I ran errands for her from time to time and came to know her well.

Her cottage was completely traditional, from the roses round the door to the herbaceous border, and the daintiest curtains to the garden gnomes fishing around the miniature pond. Mrs Jackson regularly arranged the altar flowers in the church, and was also responsible for a special event that had become a fixture in the social calendar of Little Ashington Under Wold – the annual children's party.

'You see, my dear Gill,' she had told me, 'nothing pleases me more than the look of delight in the dear children's eyes as they come into my sitting-room and see the spread I've laid out for them on the table.'

Yes – they were delighted, but it was more greed than appreciation of her display, although they always thanked Mrs Jackson very nicely. Sponge cakes, chocolate cakes, fruitcakes, marzipan cakes, doughnuts, jam tarts, bridge rolls, sandwiches and much, much more – all home-made and absolutely delicious. Some of the children came from the village, but most were from a rundown housing estate on the outskirts, where there was much poverty and deprivation. Mrs Jackson was nothing if not aware of modern-day problems.

'Poor little mites,' she told me. 'If their parents can't afford to give them a treat then surely I can.'

The vicar beamed and rubbed his hands, making a little speech at the end of each feast. 'Well, children, I think we should all give three cheers for kind Mrs Jackson and her scrumptious teas. They've become quite a tradition, haven't they? And what a spread they are –'

The cheers were always deafening and Mrs Jackson flushed with pleasure.

But there was only one drawback, one spectre at the feast, and that was Billy Baxter. He never cheered, never clapped, never said thank you. Shaped like a ferret, with a long chin and tiny eyes, Billy was dressed shabbily and was generally considered to be the most deprived of the deprived. He was also exceptionally rude, and several times when Mrs Jackson had gently chided him for his appalling table manners he had called her an 'old git'. But all she ever said was, 'He's such a sad little boy and I gather his mother is on her own. We *must* make allowances, mustn't we, Gill?'

Billy Baxter, however, did seem to have it in for Mrs Jackson, and he ran a real campaign of hatred against her. Maybe he thought she was patronizing, maybe he didn't like being reprimanded, maybe he thought she was a snob, but he continually gave her considerable doses of verbal abuse.

One day, on the way back to school, I ran into Billy lurking outside the newsagents. 'Buy me some sweets,' he whined.

'Buy your own,' I said sternly.

'I'm poor.'

'Get a job.'

'Too young.'

'Run some errands.'

'Like you do for that old git Jackson?'

'She's not an old git,' I replied clearly and calmly, as if he was very stupid. 'Mrs Jackson is a very generous lady.'

Billy picked his nose and examined the contents with interest.

I decided that this was not a conversation I was going to continue, so I tried to push past him, but Billy resisted, and although I was much bigger than he was I didn't want to run the risk of the embarrassment of having a shoving match with him in public.

'Get out of the way,' I said.

'Only if you buy me some sweets.'

'I'll buy you a razor-blade if you'll cut your throat.'

'Shove off.'

'I will,' I said, turning away furiously. 'I'll come back when the pavement isn't blocked by a rat.'

Feeling somehow that I had come off worse I walked off smartly back down the village street to a torrent of insults from Billy. I was blinking back angry tears of humiliation, when Mrs Jackson walked brightly out of the Copper Kettle tearooms.

'Why, Gill – what's the matter?'

'Nothing.'

'But there is. You're crying.' She glanced up and down the street, and then Mrs Jackson's eyes rested on Billy's retreating back as he pushed his way into the newsagents. She turned back to me, full of understanding, but all she said was, 'We must make allowances, mustn't we?'

For the life of me I couldn't think why. Billy was just selfish and ill-mannered. What was more, I found myself almost jealous of Mrs Jackson's tolerance.

'Hello, dear.' It was the day before the annual party and I knocked on Mrs Jackson's damson-painted door to see if I could be of any help. She was looking sprightly and wearing an apron embroidered with rabbits. Her hair was drawn back into a pale-blue scarf and the interior of the cottage smelt deliciously of baking.

'Do you want a hand?' I asked.

'Or two?' She smiled lovingly at me. 'Do come in and try my cheese scones. It's a new recipe and I'm not sure if it quite works.'

Of course it did – they were delicious. Standing in her pretty red-and-white kitchen, surrounded by labelled tins and jars, with crocheted texts hanging on the walls and pots and pans sparkling on the Welsh dresser, I revelled yet again in Mrs Jackson's special aura of warmth and comfort.

'Has that Baxter boy been troubling you again, dear?'

'Not a lot,' I lied.

'Are you sure?'

'Oh, he's just a pain. I can handle him.'

'He's just one of God's little children, after all. Of course, I've had to speak to Billy about his unfortunate habit of picking his nose, but I only mean it for the best. It *is* so unhygienic.'

'What did he say to you?' I asked warily.

'Oh, I couldn't tell you that, dear. It's far too unpleasant.'

'I'll fix him.'

'Oh no.' She gave me a warm, ungrudging smile.
'I'm sure he'll soon see the error of his ways. Now – I
want to tell you about my centrepiece.'

Mrs Jackson's party-table centrepieces were legendary,
and the vicar had called them 'overwhelming'. Still, that
was the vicar – he made everything sound larger than
life. Every year she created something different: a huge
chocolate chicken, a monster jelly in the shape of one of
Cinderella's ugly sisters, an immense gingerbread cottage, an ice-cream mountain with a train running
through it; a spaceship made of marzipan. So I waited
with anticipation for news of what the latest one was to
be.

'Here we are.' She went to a cupboard and produced
a large cap with a bell on top.

'What's that for?' I asked.

'Don't you recognize little Noddy's hat?' Mrs Jackson
gave me a merry smile. 'I'm going to make a giant head
out of cake – fruitcake – and I shall decorate it with
icing sugar, marzipan, glacé cherries and hundreds and
thousands. Do you think the kiddies will like that?'

'Of course they will,' I said fervently. 'It's a lovely idea.'

A little later we both walked down to the village shop.
It was late on Saturday afternoon and the sun was still
high in a glorious July sky. As we approached the duck
pond, Mrs Jackson produced bread from her wicker
basket and, as usual, began to scatter chunks on to the
water. The ducks arrived in a flurry and soon the air
was raucous with their cries. Then I heard a nasal voice.

'Fancy wasting bread on them lot.'

I wheeled round to see Billy Baxter, his lips parted in a goading leer.

'What do you want?'

'Nothing.'

He looked even more ferret-like than ever.

'Why don't you push off then?' I asked him.

'Just watching Lady Muck get rid of her leftovers,' he said casually.

I had a sudden longing to shove Billy in the pond, so I grabbed his shirt and held him at arm's length while he tried to kick me. Good thing I'm so tall.

Just as he was swearing at me, Mrs Jackson, who had apparently been lost in thought, swung round on us and said, 'Let him go, dear.'

'But –'

'Let him go.'

I did as she told me and he stood there glowering at us, too surprised and frightened to take a running kick at me as he would have liked to. Instead, Billy contented himself with renewed abuse.

'You should be arrested,' he said.

'Why's that, Billy?' asked Mrs Jackson gently.

'You let *her* beat me up.'

'I don't think she's hurt you.'

'She assaulted me – tore my shirt. Look.' He pulled at a hole, making it bigger. 'It's the only one I got.'

'Clear off,' I yelled, making tracks for Billy again. This time I'd get him by the throat, I promised myself.

But Mrs Jackson raised a hand. 'Please leave him,' she said. I paused, while she inspected Billy Baxter rather as if he were a Victorian waif. 'Listen,' she said to him. 'Why don't you do something useful?'

'Who? Me?' He seemed aghast.

'Yes,' she said firmly. 'Why don't you come home

with me and give me a hand with the party preparations for tomorrow – and maybe sample some of the food I'm preparing. Just to tell me how it tastes.'

I stood there in silence, completely stunned as I saw my own role suddenly taken over by Billy. Why was she doing this?

Mrs Jackson turned back to me with one of her most understanding smiles. 'I know Billy is very rude . . .'

'Oi –' he began, but then remembered the food and kept quiet.

'But he hasn't had the chances other little boys have had, have you, Billy?'

'No, miss,' he replied demurely.

I could have thrown up.

'So I'll see you tomorrow, Gill. I do hope you can come and help.'

'I'll see if I've got time,' I said, stiff with offence.

'I've got a little surprise, dear – specially for you and for me, so I hope you will be able to come along.'

As they walked off together, I saw that Billy had taken her arm and was helping her along. The sight both infuriated me and made me jealous at the same time.

I slept badly that night, for I kept dreaming of Billy yelling at Mrs Jackson – and the old lady taking it, whilst she carried a great big tray of doughnuts with the jam welling out of them into her sitting-room.

The next afternoon, feeling tired and left-out, I went round to Mrs Jackson's cottage at the appointed time. The children were noisily gathered round the huge spread, the vicar was talking cheerfully to them and not being listened to, and Mrs Jackson was clattering about in the kitchen, singing a sweet and uplifting hymn, as she often did when she was preparing a treat.

I knocked on the door. 'Can I come in?' I asked hesitantly.

'Wait a minute, dear.'

'Have you got Billy in there with you?'

'I certainly have. Just go into the sitting-room and I'll bring in my centrepiece.'

Dutifully, but with considerable ill-feeling, I did as I was told.

The vicar was saying jovially, 'Now, children, shall we all be little dogs and say bow-wow?'

'Bow-wow!' they all shouted noisily.

'And little cats and say miaow.'

'Miaow!' they wailed, with considerable increase in volume.

'And little donkeys and say ee-aw.'

'Ee-aw!'

The vicar came over to my side. 'Now I wonder what's keeping the good Mrs Jackson – she of the busy hands and the kind heart?'

'I don't know,' I replied dully.

'I'm afraid my abilities as an entertainer are running thin,' he confessed.

'So sorry to keep you waiting.' Mrs Jackson was slightly flustered. 'I've just been arranging my centrepiece. Now – let's turn the lights out, shall we?'

'Mrs Jackson,' I ventured.

'Yes, dear?'

'Are you feeling quite well?' Her face was flushed, perspiration was standing out on her forehead and her eyes were feverishly staring ahead. Did she have flu? Could she have been drinking? And where was the wretched Billy Baxter?

'Are you ready, children?'

'Yes!' they yelled.

'Vicar?'

'I'm ravenous, Mrs Jackson,' he confessed.

'I'm so glad. Just one minute.' She disappeared back into the kitchen and then returned bearing Noddy's head on a big silver tray. 'I do hope you like this, children.'

The clapping and cheering began, but quickly trickled away and the vicar whispered something indistinguishable. Then I took a closer look. I don't remember much more except that it must have been my screams that started everyone else off.

It wasn't Noddy's head on the tray after all, surrounded by so many glowing candles. Billy Baxter was there instead – his mouth wide open in a permanent scream and the bloodied stump of his neck ruffled in coloured paper.

I hadn't realized how much Mrs Jackson hated him.

The group round the crackling flames of the campfire were silent with shock.

'It's amazing how many weird people there are out there,' said Jules, a Haitian living in London. 'Let me tell you about Madame Simone. She practises voodoo from her flat in South London.'

6

VOODOO

Marie-Denise was terrified of the joyriders who screeched their stolen cars around the Bloxham Estate in South London at night. She was eleven, and her parents had gone back to Haiti because there was some trouble at home, so her gran was looking after her and the twins. She wasn't so much worried about herself – it was Jean-Luc and Duval that gave her such concern. In their parents' absence the two nine-year-olds had got completely out of control and would run round the estate late at night, despite her best efforts to find them.

'They're devils,' Gran would pronounce, standing on the balcony of Wessex House, looking at them charging across the muddy grass of the so-called 'landscaped' area below. '*I* can't control them.'

'The trouble is,' said Marie-Denise, 'there's nothing to do here.'

Her statement was all too true. There was a large number of signs around the blocks firmly stating NO BALL GAMES, and the only official nod to the existence of children was a rusty climbing-frame and a swing that had lost its chains.

'I don't care,' replied Gran obscurely. 'Those two are heading for trouble.'

Later that evening, just as dusk was falling, Marie-Denise and Gran watched some joyriders arrive in a stolen VW Golf. They did handbrake turns, and a crowd of teenagers and children, which included the

57

twins, watched them skid the VW round with an appalling screaming of tyres.

Because the estate was rough it had become a no-go area for the police, and normally the joyriders remained unpunished. Even now they were squealing round the service roads with kids running after them, and Marie-Denise could see Jean-Luc and Duval jumping up and down in excitement.

'I'll go and get them,' she said firmly, and her gran sighed.

'You can bring them back, but they'll be out again in seconds.'

'No, they won't.'

But as Marie-Denise ran down the stairs she knew all too well that her gran was right. The boys' hours of captivity were limited. The teacher at school said they were both a 'pain', and 'what could you expect with the mother away like she is?' But what could *anyone* expect here, Marie-Denise thought as she emerged into a wilderness of graffiti-smeared concrete, grey and unending, with the rubbish piled up on the pavements, burnt-out cars in the basement garage and closed shops, protected by steel shutters. The only traders who had stayed on were the industrious family who had a newsagent and an off-licence which had expanded into a grocery. They also had shutters, which at least protected them and their merchandise from ram-raiders.

Now, as she strode towards the watching crowd, Marie-Denise felt vulnerable. She knew one of the joyriders, a bumptious and overconfident fourteen-year-old known as Terry Caxton. He continually mocked her at school, partly because she was protective towards Jean-Luc and Duval, and partly because he wanted her to notice him – which she determinedly didn't. 'Little mummy,' Terry called her, and she hated him more

than she had ever hated anyone. She always stood up to
Terry, never allowing him to get the better of her, but
this seemed to be a challenge and made him goad her
even more.

Marie-Denise pushed her way to the front of the
crowd and made an ineffective grab at Jean-Luc and
Duval but, well practised, they quickly evaded her and
ran over to the other side of the road. The brand-new,
stolen VW Golf was backing up fast, and behind the
wheel was the grinning face of Terry Caxton. What was
worse, he saw her and revved the car fiercely, showing
off, his twelve-year-old brother sitting beside him in the
passenger seat.

Then Terry's hands slipped off the wheel and he
temporarily lost control of the VW, which mounted
the pavement, scattering spectators and narrowly missing
Jean-Luc and Duval. Because they were quick-witted
and athletic, the twins managed to leap out of the way,
but it was a close thing. Terry had the car back under
control in seconds, but Marie-Denise fell into a boiling
rage. As the VW came to a halt beside her, she ham-
mered on the driver's window with her fists, screaming
at him.

Grinning provocatively, Terry wound down the glass.
'How's it going?' he asked maliciously.

'You raving idiot. You nearly killed them.'

'Little mummy.'

Speechless with fury, Marie-Denise slapped Terry
around his sallow features as hard as she could, while his
brother chortled with excitement. For once Terry
looked nonplussed, and the crowd pressed forward,
scenting trouble.

'You'll regret that,' he said, his usual bravado grin
rather automatic.

'I enjoyed it.'

'Know what your twins asked me the other day?' he sneered.

'I don't want to hear.' But Marie-Denise knew something bad was coming by the look of sudden delight in Terry's ash-grey eyes.

'They asked me if I'd take them joyriding.' His moment of triumph was complete.

'No.' A cold chill seized Marie-Denise, making her squirm with rage and fear.

'Said I'd be pleased to take them.' Terry made the dreadful idea sound like a visit to the movies.

'You can't –'

'Try and stop me.'

'Please –' At the fatal word Terry's smile became even broader, and Marie-Denise cursed herself for weakening. Now he truly had her in his power, but she was determined that she would still challenge him. 'If you do – I'll kill you.'

'Yeah?'

'I'll have you nicked.'

'Yeah?'

'I'll –' Marie-Denise ran out of words and the tears glistened in her eyes.

'If they want a ride, they can have it.' Dale, Terry's younger brother, was equally unpleasant and had a foxiness that was an additional threat. 'I know they'd enjoy it. Oi – Jean-Luc, Duval.'

They came over at once, curious and delighted to be singled out by the superheroes.

'Want to take a ride sometime?'

Their faces shone. 'You bet.'

'When?'

'You'll never go with them,' yelled Marie-Denise. 'If you do – you'll get the hiding of your lives.'

But Jean-Luc and Duval ignored her, and ran back laughing into the swelling crowd.

'Doesn't look as if big sister has too much influence,' purred Terry delightedly. 'So you're long on being mouthy, short on getting them to do what you want – right?'

'Right,' added Dale.

Marie-Denise walked away.

'You're not to go.'

'We'll do what we like,' yelled Jean-Luc.

'You'll be killed.'

'He's an ace driver,' shouted Duval.

The argument between Marie-Denise and her brothers continued with neither side giving an inch. Eventually the boys went out to play. It was Saturday and Marie-Denise had to clean the flat while her gran went shopping. When she returned she found her granddaughter in tears.

'What's happened?' she asked philosophically, used to trouble and continually bearing a load of worry. But when Marie-Denise told her the full story, she was horrified. 'They *can't* do that.'

'They might,' said Marie-Denise hopelessly. Usually such a confident person, she really felt she had lost her grip this time.

'I'll call the police.'

'What can *they* do? This is a no-go area.'

'It most certainly is *not*.' Gran was always determined to believe the estate was respectable.

'It is. And anyway, what *can* the police do? Nothing's happened yet. But it will. The twins are out of control and Terry's determined to get even with me for slapping him. Next thing we know – the twins will be dead. I can see it all.' Marie-Denise lost what little control she had left and burst into desperate sobs while Gran put her arms round her and held her close. 'What can we do?' Marie-Denise cried. 'What can we do to save them?'

'There's always Madame Simone,' Gran said slowly.

'Who?'

'Madame Simone. You know – top of Marshall House.'

'Her! She's mental.'

'Is she? She's Haitian, like us.' Gran's voice shook.

'What could *she* do? Put a spell on them?'

'She's a wise woman.'

Marie-Denise looked up into her grandmother's dark eyes, seeing centuries of old ways, old superstitions that she had never really left behind in Haiti. They had travelled with her and were still important, even though buried under years of living in Britain.

'What could she *do*?' insisted Marie-Denise.

'*I* don't know. Go and see her.'

'I haven't spoken to her since I was little. She won't recognize me.'

'Yes she will. And if she doesn't – tell her I sent you.'

'Well –'

'Go now, child. You'll only get yourself in such a state that you won't be able to cope. Besides, I'm afraid too. That boy is trouble.'

Madame Simone lived on the top, tenth floor of an old block at the back of the estate. She was very old and to Marie-Denise's knowledge hadn't been out for years. She was generally thought to be a weirdo, so Marie-Denise was both anxious and afraid as she finally knocked at the battered door. For a while no one replied, and she was just about to knock again when a gravelly voice came through the intercom.

'Who is it?'

'Marie-Denise. You know my gran, Jacqueline.'

'What you want?'

'Your advice.'

'I got no advice to give anyone.'

'Please –'

There was a long pause, after which the chain was taken off and so many security devices clicked and rattled that minutes passed as Madame Simone unlocked the gates to her fortress. Finally, the door opened and she stood on the threshold, a mountain of a woman, with a shock of black frizzy hair and pale eyes.

'You better come in.'

Madame Simone very slowly led Marie-Denise to an inner chamber that had once been the living-room of the flat and was now a bizarre cross between a witch's cavern, a chemist's and a laboratory. There was a grimness to the place that spoke of ancient alchemy, which terrified Marie-Denise. She had never been here before, and fervently wished she had never come. She must be mad expecting this crazy old lady to help her. Again Marie-Denise saw Terry's grinning face, and in her mind she heard him say, 'Now she believes in witchcraft – poor little mummy.'

'Well?'

The paraphernalia around them included glass jars with stuffed owls and crows, bottles of unidentifiable substances, dead bats, musical instruments, a row of teeth and, worse still, what appeared to be paws on a string and beetles scuttling in a cage.

There was also a scuffling sound that came from a closed door near the bookcase, which was stacked with dusty volumes displaying the signs of the zodiac.

'What's that noise?' asked Marie-Denise, startled.

'My cats,' said Madame Simone a little too quickly and defensively, or was it just Marie-Denise's imagination? 'Come on, you'd better tell me what you want.' Her voice was commanding and Marie-Denise hesitantly began to explain her problem.

When she had finished, the mountainous lady was
silent. Then she said slowly, 'You hate him – this
Terry?'

'Very much – and if he harms the twins –'

'You know how powerful hatred is?' The gravelly
voice was soft and questioning.

'Yes.'

'Hatred can be far more dangerous than your Terry's
cars.'

'He's not *my* Terry.' Marie-Denise was deeply frus-
trated.

'But you are worried about your twins.'

'Of course I am.'

Sighing, Madame Simone moved heavily to a shelf
and took down a large bottle of dark liquid with a
screw cap. 'You have to throw this in your Terry's
face.'

'What?'

'You have to throw this in his face,' she replied pa-
tiently.

'What will it do to him?'

'It will stop him.'

'You mean hurt him? I'll get nicked –' So the old
lady was crazy after all. What was in the bottle, wondered Marie-Denise. Acid?

'It won't hurt.'

'How can I be sure?'

She unscrewed the bottle and poured a little of the
dark liquid on to the dusty table in front of her. Nothing
happened.

'Now if that was acid –'

'Yes – I know. It would burn the table.' But Marie-
Denise still looked down at the liquid doubtfully.

'He'll certainly forget about driving cars.' The old
lady gave a low growl of amusement.

'And you're *sure* it won't hurt him?'

'I promise.'

'OK.' Marie-Denise took the bottle despondently. It's probably harmless, she thought. What a waste of time the visit had turned out to be. Gran was going senile. 'I must go. Thank you,' she said automatically.

'Remember about that hatred.'

'Yes?'

'It's very powerful. Can you not be friends with your Terry?'

'Never – and he's not *mine*,' Marie-Denise repeated fiercely.

'You really *do* hate him, don't you?' said the old lady sadly.

'Look what he might do to the twins.'

Madame Simone nodded and then began to move towards the door. She took Marie-Denise's hand and her grip was hot and moist, as if she had a fever.

'You'll try to love him –'

'No way.'

'And only use the bottle if there's an emergency – an emergency that might mean death.'

'I'll be careful.' Marie-Denise suddenly wanted to get out of the claustrophobic confines of the flat as quickly as possible. She could hear a kind of bumping, shuffling sound behind that closed door; Madame Simone must have absolutely hundreds of cats in there, she thought, and suddenly felt sick as she imagined the dusty, fur-ridden atmosphere in the little room. 'Thank you – I'll – I'll be in touch,' she said, meaning never to see the old woman again.

'You know where I am if you need me. Only open the bottle in the greatest emergency.' Her voice was forbidding.

★

For some days nothing happened. Marie-Denise didn't see Terry and the twins were comparatively well-behaved. But the next Friday night he returned with yet another stolen car. As she stared out of the window, Marie-Denise's heart sank. But at least the twins were safe this time, she thought, for they had gone to bed hours ago.

She was just about to go herself, when Gran came stumbling into the living room, looking distraught.

'They've gone.'

'What?'

'The twins – they must have slipped out when we were watching TV. The little devils –'

Suddenly the screaming of tyres and grinding of gears seemed much louder – almost in the flat itself. The cold feeling swept back inside Marie-Denise and she started to shake all over, partly in fear, but also in hatred. 'They've gone to Terry.'

'No –'

'Yes they have, Gran. They're down there now.' The hatred grew in her, outweighing the fear, and she ran into the bedroom, grabbing at Madame Simone's bottle of liquid and pulling on her coat. She had only told Gran that the old woman had been kind and full of advice, so she stuffed the weapon deep into her pocket.

'Where're you going?' asked Gran feebly.

'Where do you think?'

'You be careful.'

'OK.' Marie-Denise slammed the door behind her.

'It's not right,' said a girl about her own age, as Marie-Denise tried to struggle through the excited crowd.

'What isn't?' she asked, but she knew what she was going to hear.

'He's got a couple of little kids strapped in the back –

66

as well as his brother in the front. That guy's going to kill someone.'

'No, he's not,' yelled Marie-Denise, finally worming her way through the tightly pressed throng, to see Terry doing a handbrake turn in a stolen Rover. Directly he saw her he came to a squealing halt.

'Hello, little mummy.'

'Let them out.'

'I don't think they want to come.'

Sure enough the twins, excited and completely unafraid, screamed abuse at her from the back of the Rover.

Marie-Denise looked round desperately, but there were no adults in the crowd at all – just a bunch of goggling kids.

Marie-Denise's hatred for him was now so great that she felt consumed by it; dragging Madame Simone's bottle out of her coat pocket she unscrewed the top – and hurled the contents over him.

'Acid!' he yelled, and reaching out an arm to ward her off hit the bottle with such force that some of the liquid splashed back over Marie-Denise's face.

'No!' she yelled.

Wrenching open the door of the Rover, she undid the twins' seatbelts and yanked them both out while they shouted and kicked, eventually beginning to cry. Some of the older girls came to her aid, turning on Terry, who was still wiping away the liquid, belatedly accusing him of being a potential killer.

Marie-Denise paused for a second, staring at him, and he met her eyes, more puzzled than angry.

'What *is* this stuff?'

'*I* don't know.'

'Where did you get it?'

Marie-Denise didn't reply; she just stood there, staring at him, a struggling twin in each hand.

'It's sticky,' Terry muttered.

She clawed some of it away from her own face and almost lost Jean-Luc, but someone grabbed him and she was in control again, dragging them back to the flat and away from the crowd.

'Fancy taking those little kids.'

'He could have killed them.'

'Mindless idiot.'

'Poor little mites!'

'Let's get out of here, Tel,' muttered Dale, and the Rover roared into life again, taking the bend too sharply, sending a dustbin flying, and speeding off down the main road, full-beam headlights relentlessly probing the darkness.

'We were having fun – till *you* turned up.'

'You always wreck everything.'

'Shut up, you two,' snapped Marie-Denise, her grip hardening on their wrists. 'Unless you want a good hiding.'

Somehow, she dragged Jean-Luc and Duval up the long flight of stairs, while they still howled and raged at her. Her head felt strange – as if she was swimming underwater in slow-motion – and there was a buzzing in her ears.

Once she had handed over the protesting pair to Gran, Marie-Denise went to bed exhausted and slept almost at once. She felt as if she was in some great, echoing cavern, where inexplicable sounds assailed her ears and weird visions, disconnected and fragmented, kept coming and going in her mind's eye. Slowly they became more distinct and she saw – or thought she saw – a series of strange animals, almost human, that shambled round a small space. They were covered in lank fur and made a low grunting sound.

Slowly Marie-Denise woke, stiflingly hot, throwing off the bedclothes and lying on her back. She brushed a hand across her face, and gave a startled grunt. Staggering to her feet, she went to the mirror and pushed the lank hair away from her face. Part girl, part ape, part something much earlier – a horrifying mixture of all three – Marie-Denise looked like some atavistic throwback to the dawn of time. What was more, standing upright seemed painful and unnatural. She had to settle on all fours. She knew where she had to go, knew where the only possible hope lay: Madame Simone *had* to have the antidote.

Bounding on her paws, Marie-Denise managed to open the door and scuttle down the stairs. Her mind, at least, seemed to retain human thought, but blind panic consumed her. Scurrying across the worn grass outside with a jaundiced moon above her, she remembered what Madame Simone had said about hatred and then paused. Another creature was slowly moving towards her on all fours, grunting plaintively, hunched into itself. Terry was just a mass of long, lank hair. They met, staring, not wanting to touch each other, yet nevertheless tentatively pawing. Then she turned away and he followed.

Madame Simone stood in the hallway, accepting, resigned. It *was* the strength of hatred that determined how strongly the liquid acted, thought Marie-Denise. After all – she had been warned.

Madame Simone led them through the cluttered sitting-room and paused before the closed door. 'You managed to splash it on yourself too,' she said.

Marie-Denise hung her shaggy head and Terry's grunting became desperate.

'I don't have the antidote,' Madame Simone said. She

shook her head, flinging open the inner door. Marie-Denise saw the crouched shadows, stilled and wary.

'They all came to me,' said Madame Simone, 'after they had used up their hatred. All I can do is feed them, to understand.'

Marie-Denise and Terry slowly padded into the room.

'Are they still there?' asked Jamie, but he didn't want an answer. They all stared into the flames.

'I've got a Mexican pen-friend,' said Will, determined to change the subject. 'And he told me about someone who collected dogs.'

7

THE DAY OF THE DEAD

Carlos had first noticed the stranger a few minutes before
because he seemed to be carefully inspecting each head-
stone and mausoleum. He was particularly distinctive: tall,
pale and wearing black clothes, almost like a priest. There
was a large white carnation in his buttonhole and he
pushed in front of him a handcart which bore the words:

TIJUANA DOG SANCTUARY

It was the Mexican festival of the day of the dead –
a joyous occasion, with parties in the graveyards,
bands playing and tables groaning with food and drinks.
Soon sweets would be on sale in the form of sugar skulls
and skeletons, the rackety border town of Tijuana would
come raucously alive, and for a few hours Carlos would
know that the spirit of his father was near him.

Carlos's family possessed a mausoleum, but because
they were poor it was very small and the burial chamber
was now so full that the undertakers could only squeeze
in his father's coffin by placing it on the floor. Outside,
in steel frames and behind weatherproof glass, were the
photographs of his family's dead – some sepia-coloured
and faded, others much fresher. Carlos's father had died
only a few days ago and his photograph was the freshest
of all; his smiling face looked down in gentle dignity,
without a trace of the pain in which he had died.

The stranger was coming nearer, pushing his handcart
in front of him. Slowly he scrutinized each name on the

71

gravestones until he finally came upon the mausoleum and, completely ignoring Carlos, suddenly snapped his fingers together in triumph. The snapping sound was very unpleasant to hear, as if someone had broken a dead twig in half.

'Do you want something, *señor*?' asked Carlos.

'No.'

'Can I help you?'

'No.'

'Are you – do you know my family?'

'Not personally.' He looked closely at Carlos for the first time. 'Good afternoon,' he said abruptly and began to push his handcart away.

Carlos went back to his small, overcrowded apartment and helped his mother and younger brothers and sisters prepare for the carnival. But he could hardly concentrate on what he was doing and a curious sense of urgency overcame him as he began to worry about the stranger. Tijuana Dog Sanctuary? Wasn't that one of the places his father had once told him about? The thought began to obsess him and he looked at his watch. Nine, and twilight was already giving way to darkness. He felt an overpowering urge to return to the cemetery, to check that the mausoleum was safe and all was well. The fiesta would not begin until eleven at least, so Carlos knew he could slip out of the apartment, make his check and then return home in time to help load the food, the trestle-tables and the effigies of the saints into his uncle's truck.

It only took him five minutes to run back to the cemetery, but so great was Carlos's sense of urgency that he arrived puffing and panting, hardly able to get his breath. Then he saw the dogs – dozens of them. All were thin and emaciated, which was bad enough, but worse was to come. The gate of the mausoleum was hanging open.

Normally speaking, Carlos would have been afraid of so many strays, but this was his family's tomb. He pushed his way through their flea-bitten flanks and hurried on into the darkness of the interior. He had a box of matches on him and he struck one, the flame leaping in the musty space. Immediately, he saw that his father's coffin had disappeared and there was only a mass of withered flowers to mark where it had been. Who could have robbed the grave – and why? He was so deeply shocked that he could hardly think.

The disappearing coffin *must* have something to do with the mysterious stranger, but why were all these dogs here? Some were in the darkness with him even now, brushing against his legs, and there was an angry howl as he accidentally stepped on a paw. Another snarled as he pushed his way out. Then, to his amazement, he saw the stranger walking between the graves, this time without his handcart. Head down, he strode past without looking up.

'Wait!'

The stranger unwillingly turned round. 'Yes?'

'My father – his coffin has gone. He was only – only buried a few days ago. And what are these dogs doing round here? There're dozens of them.'

'Have you forgotten your father's profession?' asked the stranger.

Carlos shook his head, staring up again at the photograph and the inscription underneath:

ANDREAS MARTINEZ
CITY DOG CATCHER
1929–1993
A LOYAL AND DILIGENT PUBLIC SERVANT

'So?'

'Your father was a good man?'

'To us.' Carlos was desperately trying to force out the knowledge that he had always kept in the back of his mind.

'He was not a good man to the dogs.'

'No?'

'He put them in a compound – he never fed them. Many died.'

'I see.' How could the father he knew as a good, kind man do something like that? But then why should Carlos believe the stranger? For the first time, he looked up into the man's eyes. They were a liquid brown.

'You run the dog sanctuary, do you?' Carlos asked fearfully.

'I help.'

Then Carlos noticed something else about the stranger. He had an almost canine look to him, with his long nose and lean body, his rather bent-forward way of walking and his low, rather harsh voice. He laughed a low, barking sound. 'You might say I have had a dog's life.'

'I don't understand –'

'Reincarnation,' said the man softly. 'We remember little flashes of our other lives – if we believe, that is.' He paused. 'I can remember the scents of the city, and of the seashore. I can see my companions running beside me, sometimes in twos or threes, sometimes in a pack. I can hear the insults of the humans – the sharp pain of their kicks.'

'You were –'

'A stray? I've always been a stray. This life is no different from the previous one. I gravitated naturally to the sanctuary.' He paused. 'The dogs are starving there too.'

A horrible thought came into Carlos's mind. He tried to reject it but found that it kept returning – an impossible, barbaric idea. He remembered reading in a newspaper a few months ago about grave-robbing at another cemetery in Tijuana, further out of town. A number of freshly buried corpses had been taken. He looked at the white carnation in the stranger's buttonhole and saw that it was drooping a little.

'My dogs need meat,' said the stranger, 'and it is so *easy* to remove the dead – even tonight.'

'You can't –'

'The dogs come with me.'

'Please let me have my father back.' Carlos's heart thudded painfully.

'I'm often mistaken for an undertaker.'

'It's not too late, is it?'

The stranger looked intently into Carlos's eyes, but said nothing.

'*Please* let me have him back.'

'You don't know what it's like,' said the man, 'being starved and kicked.'

'My father did,' replied Carlos with a burst of anger. 'He lost his building business because his partner stole the money. He lost everything – and he had to feed eight of us. He knew what it was like to starve and be kicked around, and so do we. OK, he got the job as dog catcher and that fed us and I know how much he hated the job and I'm sorry he was bad to the animals –' Carlos ended his speech in a gabble. 'But I loved him. We *all* loved him – and we want his spirit to join us tonight.'

The stranger stared at him. Some of the strays began to whine plaintively. 'We must hurry. I have my van at the gate.' The stranger strode off and Carlos had to run to keep up with him.

'You mean you've changed your mind?'

'I can't let my dogs die.'

Carlos was thinking, Suppose he's crazy; suppose he really wants live people for meat?

Eventually they arrived at a battered van, and as they clambered in he saw the handcart wedged in the back. Carlos began to tremble.

'Don't be afraid,' the man said. 'You will be safe.'

The stranger drove to one of the poorest parts of Tijuana – a shanty town in a canyon, where hundreds of naked electric bulbs shone, powered by makeshift generators. The dogs that had followed them on the short journey from the cemetery ran in to meet others – and there was a cacophony of barking. All looked pitifully thin and mangy.

'I *had* promised myself I'd stop,' said the stranger.

'Robbing graves?'

'But what will the dogs do? They'll all die. They'll have to fend for themselves. But then I suppose I've had to do that all my life,' he added bitterly.

They drew up at a large tin shack at the end of the canyon, surrounded by desert scrub and cacti. Carlos had never been so afraid. He was certain now that the stranger was crazy and all he was doing was providing his dogs with another meal – for the first time a living one. He looked down at his bare, brown arm. There was meat there, good fresh meat.

'Don't be afraid.' The stranger put his arm round Carlos's shoulders as he opened the door of the shack. Instantly Carlos was almost overcome by the smell, but it was the sight that was the most horrific. Dozens of dogs of all possible sizes were gnawing at bones on the floor.

'Not my father –' he pleaded.

'No.'

He glanced up and saw the coffin on a broad shelf above.

'Come – we shall return the body.'

'Thank you.'

The stranger seemed immensely strong as he levered the coffin from the shelf on to the handcart, and as he began to wheel it away the dogs set up a howling that was dreadful to hear.

When the corpse had been replaced in the mausoleum the stranger offered Carlos his hand, which was warm and dry and strong.

'This is the end of my search for food. They must survive on their own now. Perhaps they'll have some luck – some of them, at least.' He paused, and then continued more rapidly. 'But I shall give them one last treat.'

'What's that?' asked Carlos.

But the stranger turned, and without looking back began to walk away past the graves, a tall, bent, already seemingly spectral figure in the night. Somewhere on the light breeze, Carlos thought he could still smell the faint scent of his carnation. A terrible thought occurred to him, but he put it to the back of his mind. '*One last treat . . .*'

The crowds gathered in Tijuana cemetery, the trestle-tables were laden with food and the band had just struck up. As couples danced around the headstones, bottles of wine were opened and a man set up a taco stand. At the same time, a child ran past him, gnawing at a sugar skeleton. In the distance Carlos could hear a distant howling. He felt the panic rising. Of course, he thought, once they had tasted warm flesh, their 'one last treat', they would want more. And where would they get it, this night of all nights? Then he saw them, swarming up the hill, their teeth bared, their mouths salivating. The dogs were coming.

'I'll never think about dogs the same way again,' shuddered Jamie.

'But you'd think you might be safe with nice ladies in tearooms, wouldn't you?' asked Tom. 'They wouldn't hurt anyone.'

'I'm not so sure now,' returned Jamie sharply. 'But tell us your story.'

8

SUNDAY ROAST

'We'll have scones, jam, fancy cakes and a pot of tea – and be quick about it.' The middle-aged woman with the powder-caked face and mascara-caked eyes was incredibly rude and even Sam, used to the shouted commands in the Nell Gwyn Tearooms, was taken aback by her tone. What was more, *this* time it was not even directed at him – for he had sometimes upset the customers by slopping tea, or even forgetting them completely – but was all too clearly designed to upset Lady Poynton.

Ever since he had taken a holiday job serving teas in the rundown old café in the high street he had felt sorry for its owner. She hadn't been there very long and was just about as hopeless at the job as Sam was.

'I'm not used to this kind of work,' she had told him when he had answered the advert. 'I'm used to, well – a better position in life.' Lady Poynton had sighed. 'But all that's over now and I'll have to get used to what I've got.'

She was an incredibly dignified figure, despite a certain all-round tattiness: tall, with snowy-white hair and aristocratic, rather spaniel-like features. Lady Poynton always wore the same outfit in the tearooms – polka-dot pinafore dress, white blouse, sensible shoes and a set of imitation pearls at her withered throat. Her whole appearance underlined the genteel state of poverty she lived in and her hands were calloused and blistered with the unaccustomed labour.

'Who's that woman then?' asked Sam as they clattered plates together in the tiny and rather bedraggled little kitchen that should have smelt of baking, but instead had the unpleasant aroma of damp dishcloths. Lady Poynton bought her cakes in — as well as the scones — and they were often hard, stale and unappetizing.

'Oh, *her*.'

'Her?'

'She's just here to crow.' She leant on the stained Formica, her lips pursed and her pale-blue eyes looking darker and angrier than he had ever seen them before. At once, Sam's heart bled for her; she was so clearly shaken and miserable.

'Crow?'

'She's the *second* Lady Poynton,' she declared.

Sam picked up the kettle and doused the two meagre teabags in the teapot. Customers sometimes complained about the strength of the tea, but Lady Poynton always said that was all she could afford. 'You mean —' he began.

'My ex-husband's married her at last. She's awful — her name used to be Jocelyn Onions and she only married him for his money. I hate her — I wish she'd roast in hell.' Lady Poynton swallowed and took a couple of her indigestion tablets. 'I'll pay her out for coming in here and mocking me in my hour of need. You see if I don't.' For a moment, all Lady Poynton's dignity had evaporated and she looked like a spiteful child. 'Gerald treated me badly — cut me off without a penny — and fought me through the courts to get his own way. He's an old man though — almost eighty now — and half crazy what with his war injuries and gout, but she — she's no more than a strumpet.'

Lady Poynton crashed the crockery together on a tray and, slapping two gloomy-looking scones, a scraping of jam and some dusty coconut cakes on to a random assortment of plates, she hurried out of the kitchen. 'I hope it all chokes her,' she muttered.

Sam peeked round the door to see the reaction of the second Lady Poynton to the unpalatable tea she was being ungraciously presented with. It wasn't long in coming.

'Why, Irene – you can do better than this.'

'It's all you're getting.'

'I'm so sorry, Mrs Pits.' The second Lady Poynton turned to her table companion, a meek-looking woman who had obviously been brought along to witness the humiliation she intended to pour on her enemy. 'This *isn't* the kind of tea I'm used to. Why – it's absolutely second-rate.' She raised her voice so that the other scattered occupants of the Nell Gwyn Tearooms could hear all too clearly what was being said. 'I mean – it's unacceptable, dear. Substandard.' She rose to her feet purposefully. 'I'll be back,' she promised.

'Back?' the first Lady Poynton echoed doubtfully. 'What are you coming back for?'

'I want to talk to you about Gerald.'

'I've nothing to do with him now.'

'I'll come back.' She looked round at the intent faces, eyes alight with curiosity. 'We need to have a little private chat.'

When the tearooms were closed, Lady Poynton broke down. Sam did his best to comfort her, but it was an impossible task for she was far too distraught to hear anything that he tried to say.

'That evil woman,' she sobbed. 'She's taken everything away from me – everything. And now all I have is this!' She looked around her miserably, and Sam saw the Nell Gwyn through her eyes: its glass fibre mock

Tudor beams, the torn lace curtains, the dusty lattice
windows and the fake inglenook where the imitation
coal fire flickered dimly yet balefully. She was dead
right; the place was a dump.

Next morning, Sam woke up with a sick headache, and
when his mother called the doctor flu was diagnosed, so
he was not able to return to the Nell Gwyn Tearooms
for four whole days. While he was ill he worried continu-
ously about poor Lady Poynton, wondering how she was
coping singlehandedly with the serving of teas and also
with her recent humiliation at the hands of Jocelyn Onions
– or the *second* Lady Poynton as she must now be known.

When he arrived at the tearooms, Sam was amazed,
for the place was packed, the tables were groaning with
unfamiliar and delicious-looking cakes, there was the
most wonderful smell of baking in the air, and there
was a queue for tables that curled out into the street.
What on earth could be going on, he wondered.

'She's got herself a new cook,' said an old man Sam
recognized as one of the few loyal customers of the old
Nell Gwyn.

'A new cook?' Sam was incredulous. How had Lady
Poynton afforded that? Normally she could hardly
scrape up the money for the tired packets of scones from
the supermarket.

'She's terrific.' There was saliva at the corner of the old
man's lips. 'She cooks like a dream. Lemon curd tarts,
gingerbread, iced buns, cream cakes –'

Sam pushed his way through into the tearooms to
avoid the remainder of the litany, and saw that although
Lady Poynton was clearly rushed off her feet she was
also enjoying every minute of her endeavours, as she
cleverly balanced a couple of trays of walnut slices and a
large marzipan cake.

'Sam. Wonderful to see you. I'm so glad you're better – and I need you more than ever. Hang on and I'll unlock the kitchen.'

'Unlock?' he exclaimed.

'Yes – Cook's in there. I mustn't let her out.' She giggled rather wildly and deposited the walnut slices on the table of a young couple who could hardly wait to attack them.

'Who *is* this cook?'

'Wait a minute, dear.' Flushed but happy, Lady Poynton took a bunch of keys from around her waist and, with a flourish, inserted the largest into a brand-new lock on the kitchen door. Sliding back a security chain, she said proudly, 'Sam – meet Cook.'

He gasped.

Clad in a boiler suit, her eyes full of terror, Jocelyn Onions, the second Lady Poynton, was lifting a tray of flapjacks from the oven. Sweating, shaking, she looked at him in mute appeal, but said nothing.

'I cut out her tongue,' explained Lady Poynton.

'*What?*'

'I cut out her tongue.' She sounded impatient now as if he was deliberately misunderstanding her. 'I couldn't bear the shouting when I dragged her down here and told her what she had to do – to show she was sorry.'

'Sorry?'

'Yes, dear. Why do you keep repeating everything? You know how she humiliated me in front of all my customers. Of course, that was nowhere near as bad as poaching my husband. So she had to repent. I got my kitchen scissors and went snip, snip, snip – and I put the pieces in the dustbin. Pieces of her tongue, dear.' Lady Poynton smiled sweetly. 'Do you understand me?'

'Yes,' stammered Sam. 'I believe I do.' And when he looked into those pale-blue eyes, he knew that Lady Poynton had gone stark raving mad.

'Now – if you're feeling quite well you'll have to help me out, dear. I've been rushed off my feet. I'll say one thing for her – she can cook!'

'Yes,' muttered Sam, grabbing a tray, 'she certainly can.' He hurried out into the tearooms, trying to think what he should do. Of course it was obvious – he should phone the police immediately, have the second Lady Poynton rescued, and the first taken away by some men in white coats. It was his duty. But despite all the urgent and convincing reasons, Sam hesitated. How would she get on in the nut-house? Surely she would be even more lonely and depressed, and there was no doubt that she would be in for life. But then there was Jocelyn Onions. Unpleasant and vindictive though she was, she hadn't deserved any of this.

Sam dithered for another few minutes and then decided to phone the police. Placing another tray of tea and delicious-looking gingerbread on table six to rapturous acclaim, he moved towards the door of the Nell Gwyn Tearooms. There was a phone-box further down the street. He would make the call and wait for the police. Sam hoped they would come very quickly indeed, for he was afraid that Lady Poynton might hole herself up in the kitchen with her speechless rival, conducting a seige while cutting off more bits of her.

'Good morning.'

'Er –'

The man was large and florid, dressed in heavy pin-stripes, and wearing a tie that had pretensions to being old school but wasn't. He looked like a plain-clothes policeman. Perhaps he is, thought Sam hopefully. Maybe someone else had seen Jocelyn Onions in the kitchen.

'I want to see Lady Poynton.'

'Which one?' blurted out Sam.

'The lady who runs these tearooms.'

84

'Ah.'

'Is she available?'

'Er – yes. You from the police?'

'No – my name is Dangerfield – George Dangerfield. I'm a Health and Safety Officer and these tearooms are on my rota for this morning.' There was a short silence. 'I need to inspect the kitchens.' Mr Dangerfield spoke slowly and loudly as if he thought Sam was an idiot.

'Oh no.'

'What?'

'I'm afraid you can't go down there now,' said Sam.

'But I must, you silly little boy. It's the law of the land. I *must* be admitted.' He began to look apoplectic, his Adam's apple protruding and swelling under his shirt collar as if it was a time bomb.

'I'll have to speak to Lady Poynton.'

'Please do – and hurry.'

But Sam didn't have to hurry. Lady Poynton was advancing on them both, a withered smile on her face.

'Can I help you?' Her voice was slightly shrill and her unfocused eyes stared straight ahead.

Mr Dangerfield explained, with great pomp and circumstance, but Lady Poynton didn't seem in the least put out. 'May I ask you to give me five minutes – just so my assistant can finish baking?'

'I can quite easily view –'

'I'm sure you can,' Lady Poynton replied very smoothly, 'but she's the nervous type and anyway she's just coming off duty.'

'Very well – I must say, a cup of tea would be most welcome.' Mr Dangerfield sniffed the air appreciatively. 'Something smells delicious.'

'That'll be our apple and cinnamon cakes. Will you try one? Or even two?'

'That would be delicious.' Mr Dangerfield edged his

large frame towards a corner table. Meanwhile, Sam wondered what to do. Should he tell Mr Dangerfield about Lady Poynton's grisly secret, or should he still make for the phone-box?

'Come on, Sam,' said Lady Poynton briskly. 'Don't hover.' She turned to Mr Dangerfield. 'He's a good boy, but he hasn't been very well.' She gave him a big, wide, friendly smile. 'Let's make sure our guest is happy and settled,' she shouted above the chatter in the tea-rooms. 'We'll be serving lunches soon.' She turned to Sam, her smile widening at his look of surprise. 'This is an innovation; we only used to have damp quiche, as Sam called it – but now, just wait till you smell it.'

In fact, after Mr Dangerfield had been served tea and cakes at the small corner table, Lady Poynton kept him waiting for quite a long time. When Sam tried to return to the kitchen he found the door locked and when he knocked on the frosted glass, Lady Poynton shouted out, 'Not now, Sam – I'm busy.'

'But –'

'Go and take some more cakes to Mr Dangerfield – I put some out on the side for you.'

'But –' Sam began again.

'Collect the bills, give the change and start taking luncheon orders.'

'There's no menu.'

'That's because there's only one dish. A roast.'

'Well,' said Mr Dangerfield. 'Those cakes were truly delicious. I'm afraid I've been a little – self-indulgent.'

'How many did you have?' asked Sam, his voice shaking nervously as he picked up the bill.

'Six – I'm afraid.' He looked embarrassed as he paid up. Then Mr Dangerfield rose stiffly to his feet and looked at his watch. 'I really *must* make my inspection now or I'll be late for my next appointment.'

'I'll see if Lady Poynton's ready,' said Sam.

'I'll come with you.'

They both walked over to the kitchen door and Sam knocked again on the frosted glass.

'Yes?' Her voice was light and sunny.

'Mr Dangerfield's here.'

'Good.'

'Are you ready?' Sam's voice wobbled and he cleared his throat.

'Quite ready, thank you.' Lady Poynton unlocked the kitchen door and stood back. Her face was slightly flushed and there were little beads of perspiration on her forehead.

The smell of roasting meat was very intense now and Mr Dangerfield's nose began to twitch with pleasure again.

'That's a very – pleasant aroma,' he announced, and despite the cakes he looked even hungrier than he had before.

'Why don't you stay to lunch?' asked Lady Poynton very sweetly.

'But I've got an appointment –'

'You can use the phone. Say you've been delayed.'

'Well –'

'Lamb's on the menu. With mint sauce and new potatoes –'

'Ah.'

'A special gravy. Buttered carrots –'

'Yes –'

'And a beautiful treacle tart to follow. Now, what do you say, Mr Dangerfield? It'll be on the house, of course – and served just after your inspection. All I ask is that you don't open the big oven – the flavour of the lamb's ruined if any air gets in. I have to get it *just* right. I mean – lamb's *so* delicate, isn't it?'

Mr Dangerfield looked round the small but scrupulously clean room with pleasure. 'This really is a delightful kitchen.' He began to poke around. 'So small yet so clean.'

And Lady Poynton simply smiled.

There was a long silence after Tom's story. The group by the lake were completely motionless.

Jamie looked at his watch. It was getting late.

'We've time for one last story,' Hannah said uneasily. 'Whose turn is it?'

'Mine.' Grant looked shifty. 'Based on someone I know.'

'Who?' asked April curiously.

'Teacher at school we used to send up a bit.'

9

BAITING MR BENSON

Mr Benson, one of the English teachers at Garwood Comprehensive, had a problem, and it was a problem that wouldn't go away. However much he tried, he couldn't keep control, and as the years rolled away, somehow it got worse. Unfortunately he also *looked* as if he couldn't keep control. He had a small, round, hesitant-looking face, with big eyes that always seemed to be wide open in mute appeal – and a lower lip that trembled. His voice was low-key, rather flat and definitely unassertive, and his clothes were downbeat – sports jackets with leather elbows and cuffs, frayed collars and dull ties, grey trousers, grey socks and brogues. He had no children of his own, but was married to a maths teacher at the same school – a stringy woman who looked like a question mark.

When Grant – I'll use my own name – and his ferret-like friend Nathan first came to Garwood from their primary school, they were well-briefed on Mr Benson. 'Good for a laugh', 'Nice wind-up', 'Total prat' were just some of the phrases that had been passed down to them by older brothers and friends, so when they arrived for their first lesson, there was a good deal of competition as to who was going to kick off the persecution first. Grant already had a macho reputation to live up to and was determined to get off to a good start, so when Mr Benson took the roll-call Grant tried to shine straight away.

'Jackson.'

'Who?'

'Jackson.' Mr Benson's voice was weary.

'Snackson,' Grant readily improvised, to the odd titter.

'Who?' asked Mr Benson in bewilderment, while the titters increased.

'Snackson.'

'I thought your name was Jackson.'

'Well, it ain't. It's Snackson.'

'It's down here as Jackson.' Mr Benson sounded worried.

'That's wrong.'

'And your first name is – is Grant?'

'Snarnt.'

'What?'

'Snarnt Snackson.'

'I don't understand.'

'I've got a cold, sir.'

'I'm sorry to hear that.'

'That's why I'm Snackson.'

There was wild laughter now. 'I thought you – er – said your – er – name *was* Snackson.'

'It is.'

The confusion lasted a little longer, the laughter increased, and Mr Benson was discomforted. He grew even more discomforted as the term progressed and Grant, backed by Nathan, asserted himself as class clown. He thoroughly enjoyed the role. Baiting Mr Benson became the central focus of Grant's world, and each day he hit a little harder and scored more effectively. Then at the beginning of the next term, Mr Benson went sick and a supply teacher arrived – and stayed. She was tough – unable to be goaded – and dealt effectively with Grant, Nathan and other troublemakers by placing them in detention.

After a couple of weeks of this unpleasant regime the headmaster made an announcement in assembly – and Grant's heart sank. 'Mr Benson sadly has had a nervous breakdown and won't be returning this term. We shall be sending a card and flowers and, of course, anyone who wishes to send him a greeting should ask the secretary for his address.'

Grant cheered up, but only a little, for the sudden idea that came into his head was scant compensation for not being able to persecute Mr Benson every day in class.

'I'm going to send a card,' Grant told Nathan later in the playground. 'It'll be quite a surprise.'

'Why's that then?' asked Nathan uneasily. He was already feeling guilty about Mr Benson's breakdown, all too aware how much he must have contributed personally.

'I just want to remind him I'm still around,' said Grant. 'So I wrote him this.' He produced a scruffy hand-drawn card which read: GREETINGS. I HAVEN'T FORGOTTEN YOU. GET BETTER SOON. I'M WAITING FOR YOU BACK AT SCHOOL. Underneath the words was a crude drawing of the class, Grant standing up and Mr Benson banging his own head against the blackboard.

'I don't think he'll like that,' said Nathan, his unease growing.

'I don't want him to,' replied Grant.

Two days later, the headmaster made another announcement in assembly. 'I'm sure you will all be very sorry to hear that Mr Benson fell off Highwater Bridge into the river last night. Fortunately he was seen and rescued by a passer-by and I'm happy to say that he's expected to make a full recovery. However, he will naturally be away rather longer than we originally anticipated.'

'Fall?' said Nathan later. 'I reckon he jumped, don't you?'

'He even made a mess of trying to top himself,' said Grant unmoved. 'Maybe I should send him another card.'

'You *can't* do that.' Nathan was very agitated now.

'Why not?'

'Because – maybe that's why he jumped. The other card –'

'Rubbish.' Grant was adamant. 'He's just an old woman.'

Nathan said nothing.

'Look at this.' Grant passed Nathan the second card on his way home from school. It showed Mr Benson jumping off the bridge and plunging into the water. The caption read: *LEARN TO DIVE. I'M STILL WAITING.*

For once, Nathan was insistent. 'You can't send that.'

'Why not?'

'It's sick – and so are you.' He tried to grab the card, but Grant held it aloft, running down the road towards the postbox, pushing it into an envelope and shoving it through the slit with a cry of triumph.

'You'll kill him,' yelled Nathan.

'He hasn't got the bottle,' replied Grant.

'What's the matter with you, Grant? Why are you so weird? So unhappy?' Nathan asked.

Grant scowled. 'I'm fine.'

'You're not. It's your folks again, isn't it?'

'Mind your own business.'

Nothing happened for the next few weeks. There were no more announcements from the head, and to Nathan's relief Grant showed no sign of posting anything either.

Time passed and there was still no news of Mr Benson. Meanwhile, Grant seemed to have been distracted by an interest in the climbing-wall of the gym, which had just been built and which simulated a hard rock climb. Both Grant and Nathan had first become interested in this kind of challenge when they had been at a school camp last year. They had even gone to the extent of buying some equipment and practising several times at a sandstone rock face a few miles out of town, but baiting Mr Benson had become such a major preoccupation to Grant that he had lost all interest in climbing, so Nathan was glad to see that this was being revived – even if as obsessively as he had persecuted his teacher.

He would throw himself at the simulation, inching his way up limpet-like on the surface, somehow managing to jam his hands and feet into the smallest and most unlikely crannies. After a couple of months he succeeded in climbing higher than any other pupil in the class and, walking home, Nathan congratulated him, hoping this new passion would make him forget Mr Benson.

'Dad's walked,' he admitted unexpectedly. 'And Mum's drunk most nights.'

'Do you want to come over to my place?' asked Nathan.

'No. Got to look after the old girl, haven't I?'

'Yeah. But the climbing's good –'

'I think of Dad when I do it. I can see him a bit further up the simulation – always above me.'

'You trying to get to him?'

'I'm trying to pull him off,' snapped Grant. 'He's right out of order. You ought to see what he did to Mum before he left. Beat her up, didn't he?' He paused, and Nathan waited, suddenly feeling much older. 'It's funny –'

'What is?'

'I don't want to wind up Benson any more.'

'Why?'

'Not since Dad left. He used to remind me of him.'

'Benson?'

'Not to look at really, but Dad was like a wimp when he was sober although he was a real tiger when he was drunk. Funny thing is – I could never get a reaction out of Dad like I did with Benson. Do you get me?'

Nathan wasn't quite sure that he did. Suddenly, he froze.

'What's up?' asked Grant.

'That was him.'

'Who?'

'Benson.'

'But he's in the nut-house.'

'Wasn't he a voluntary patient?' Nathan said, looking deeply shocked. 'I saw him over there – on the other side of the road.'

'Rubbish.'

'I *did*.'

They both craned their necks so that they could see into the crowd in the busy teatime high street.

'Can't see him,' Grant scoffed.

'He's disappeared.'

'Yeah?'

'I told you.' Nathan was insistent. 'I saw Benson. It was definitely him.'

'You must have been mistaken.'

'Maybe.' Nathan's air of conviction suddenly evaporated.

Grant and Nathan lived on the same estate – a huge grey area of concrete, smeared by dogs and graffiti. A big adventure playground had been built on the central square, and it was packed with kids just out of school, running up and down the catwalks, swinging from ropes and frames. Normally Grant and Nathan used the playground for climbing practice.

'Want a go on the big net?' asked Grant.

'I'll have to put on my jeans,' Nathan began. 'Mum said I mustn't – wait –'

'What's up?'

'He's in there.'

'Who?'

'Benson.'

'You going crazy?'

'Look for yourself.'

But Grant didn't have to. Mr Benson, looking far more confident than they had ever seen him, walked briskly out of the playground. He gave them a cheerful, confident wave, got into a rather fast-looking Renault, and drove off.

'Blimey,' said Grant.

'It's weird.' Nathan stared after the speeding car. 'I mean – he *looks* different. Less of a wimp. More confident – and he was wearing jeans. He looked like – like a –'

'He looked like my dad,' muttered Grant.

They saw Mr Benson again and again that evening, and each time they did so, Grant and Nathan felt a bemused sense of shock gradually turning into fear. They saw him while they were on their bikes outside the supermarket, in a queue at the cinema, sauntering along a back lane, and later jogging past Nathan's house in a track suit.

'He doesn't even *live* round here,' said Grant wonderingly. 'What's he doing?'

'Watching us?'

'Why should he do that?'

'Haven't a clue.' Nathan tried to sound casual but failed. 'Why don't you speak to him?'

'Me?' Grant was outraged.

'Yeah. Ask him what he's doing. Ask him if he's watching us.' Nathan's voice was shrill.

'No way.'

'You've got to!'

'I'm going home,' said Grant firmly. 'I've got Mum to look after.'

But looking after Mum was impossible. When he got home he found her crying fit to burst, and then she went off to the pub. Grant went to bed and then woke up halfway through the night, convinced that he had heard something rattling against the window. The sound came again and he recognized it as a pebble. Nathan must be outside.

He pulled up the window sharply. 'Oi!'

'Yes, Grant?'

'What are *you* doing?' he asked, seeing Mr Benson.

'Taking a walk.'

'You don't live round here.'

'No – but I find my steps keep dragging me in this direction.' Mr Benson was leaning up against a lamppost, wearing a trendy anorak. 'We won't talk long – I don't want to wake everyone up.'

'What do you want?'

'Nothing.'

'Why are you watching us?' he tried again, his voice trembling.

'I'm not watching, Grant. I'm waiting.'

'Waiting? What for?'

'I'm waiting for you.'

'And then he pushed off,' Grant told Nathan the next

96

day. It was a Saturday, and they had decided to go climbing.

'What was he *doing*?'

'Trying to scare us, I s'pose.'

'Do you think he's crazy?' whispered Nathan.

'No,' replied Grant firmly. 'I've never seen him looking so good.'

The rock outcrop was a local phenomenon – huge sandstone crags, some with a sheer ascent. There were easy climbs and hard climbs, and right now the one Grant and Nathan were making for was one that was somewhere in between the two. Nathan enjoyed climbing and the boys worked well together, but for Grant it had become very special indeed. The challenge, the dwarfing rocks, the physicality, all shut out the terrible rows at home, the drunkenness and now the emptiness, with his mother weeping and, after the pub, staggering up the stairs to her lonely bedroom and sleepless nights.

'Let's get up Heather Ridge,' he said suddenly. 'We've never done that before.'

'It's tough,' said Nathan.

'We can do it.'

Roped together, they began to ascend, looking intently for handholds and footholds. Sweat began to pour down their faces in the fierce sunlight, but gradually the sky became overcast and there was a hint of thunder in the sultry heaviness.

'You OK?' asked Grant, who had taken the lead.

'Sure. You?'

'I'm fine – it's just this weather. It's like wading through treacle.'

They climbed on until they were just under the overhang, where they paused for a breather. It looked dauntingly steep, but Grant pulled himself over, leaving Nathan on the narrow ledge below. Struggling, panting a little, Grant knelt on the wiry grass and prepared to help Nathan up, but before he could do so he heard a quiet, friendly voice.

Mr Benson was smiling and leaning against a tree. He was dressed in brand-new slimline jeans, an open shirt and denim jacket. 'Hello.'

'Er –'

'I know you enjoy climbing.' He began to stroll over to Grant.

'I – I didn't think – you'd be here.' Grant could have kicked himself for sounding so stupid.

'I like to take an interest in your activities, Grant. It gives me something to do. Time hangs a bit heavy since I've been ill.' He looked around him. 'Like the air – like Nathan so secure on your rope.'

'What's going on?' yelled Nathan from below.

'Hang on,' Grant shouted back.

Mr Benson chuckled. He was now centimetres away from Grant and there was something in his eyes – something different that instinctively convinced Grant that Nathan had been right. Mr Benson was crazy.

Mr Benson passed Grant and stared down at Nathan on his precarious ledge. 'Pull him up.'

Slowly, rather unsteadily, Grant did as he was told, and soon Nathan was standing on Heather Ridge, looking up hypnotically into the intense eyes of Mr Benson. Stiffly, both boys tried to edge forward, but a voice they hardly recognized, low and angry and ferocious, told them to stop where they were and not to move.

'You've got to listen now, haven't you?'

They stared at him uncomprehendingly.

'You've got to listen now – for the first time in your lives.'

Nathan nodded, but Grant's head didn't move.

'Still defying me, Grant?'

An image of his father flashed through his mind.

'You've got no right –'

'I've got every right. You prey on my mind – that's why I've been following you – waiting for my opportunity. I've been through hell and back because of you, Grant. Even my wife left me. And then I got your cards. Not very nice cards, were they?'

'A joke –' Grant began.

'That's right,' stuttered Nathan, his voice shrill and pleading. 'It was only a joke.'

'Poor taste.'

'Yeah – we're sorry.'

'Very, very poor taste. But I'm going for a new image now, boys. Have you noticed my clothes?'

'Nice,' sniffed Nathan.

'I shall be going back to school in my new clothes. And when I get back it's all going to be different. But there's just one little thing I need to do first.'

As if reading his mind, Nathan wailed, 'We'll see you at school, Mr Benson. And you're right – it will be different. We'll treat you with respect, won't we, Grant?'

But Grant didn't say anything.

Mr Benson smiled his mad smile. 'I don't think Grant will ever do that, will you, Grant? Despite my new image.'

There was a dreadful silence and then Grant began to laugh. A combination of fatigue and hysteria swept over him. All he could see was his father's wimpish, sober face in Mr Benson's new clothes.

'Stop laughing, Grant,' yelled Nathan.

But he couldn't, and the sound of his raucous, almost sobbing merriment echoed around the rocks.

'You're not listening to me again, are you, Grant? You're not listening to a word I say.' The smile fixed on his face, Mr Benson moved like a panther, shoving them both in the chest and sending Nathan and Grant plunging over the abyss.

'It was *you*, wasn't it?' said Jamie at last. 'The story was about *you*.'

Grant was silent. 'I was in hospital for over a year. Nathan died.' Tears were pouring down his cheeks and he shivered uncontrollably in the cold night air.

'What about Mr Benson?'

'He's in the nut-house.'

'Will they ever let him out?' asked April fearfully.

'Maybe — one day.' Grant looked towards the safety of the house and then back at the moor. Was that a figure walking towards him? He gazed at the white-faced group, huddled round the ashes of the fire. 'Let's go back,' he said.

THE FOX OF SKELLAND
Rachel Dixon

Samantha's never liked the old custom of Foxing Day – the fox costume especially gives her the creeps. So when Jason and Rib, children of the new publicans at The Fox and Lady, find the costume and Jason wears it to the fancy-dress disco, she's sure something awful will happen.

Then Sam's old friend Joseph sees the ghost of the Lady and her fox. Has she really come back to exact vengeance on the village? Or has her appearance got something to do with the spate of burglaries in the area?

THE SHADOW-CAGE AND OTHER TALES OF THE SUPERNATURAL
Philippa Pearce

Quite ordinary things turn out to be haunted in the world Philippa Pearce creates – a funny little statue, an old biscuit barrel, a nursery cupboard – and in quite ordinary circumstances. Memories of past unhappiness can cling to a place connected with them. A man out for his evening exercise can find his hatred of his brother suddenly taking shape as a running companion. And human passions can even reach beyond the grave if they're powerful enough – a mother's longing for her daughter's return, an old man desperate at the neglect of his once-cherished garden. These ten stories are written with all the fine perception for which their author is celebrated.

ANASTASIA MORNINGSTAR
Hazel Hutchins

If Sarah and Ben hadn't been in the grocery store that day, they wouldn't have seen Derek Henshaw trying to steal a water pistol. And they wouldn't have seen him being turned into a frog by the woman who worked there. Anastasia Morningstar looked quite ordinary (and she certainly had a very ordinary job) but Sarah and Ben soon learned that she could do some very *extraordinary* things . . .

THE WEATHER WITCH
Paul Stewart

Clee Manor is hardly the kind of place that young Londoners Kerry and Joe want to spend the summer. But as direct descendants of the sixteenth-century witch who was responsible for the disappearance of the village of Cleedale, they find themselves drawn into the house's mysterious past.

It is only when they discover the long-lost village and encounter the Weather Witch herself, however, that they begin to understand the danger and awesome power they face.